Eager For More
(EagerBoyz 2)

H.L Day

Other books by H.L Day

EagerBoyz series
Eager To Try (EagerBoyz 0.5)
Eager For You (EagerBoyz 1)
Eager For More (EagerBoyz 2)

Too Far series
A Dance too Far (Too Far #1)
A Step too Far (Too Far #2)

Temporary Series
A Temporary Situation (Temporary; Tristan and Dom #1)
A Christmas Situation (Temporary; Tristan and Dom #1.5)
Temporary Insanity (Temporary; Paul and Indy #1)

Fight for Survival series
Refuge (Fight for Survival #1)

Standalones
Time for a Change
Kept in the Dark
Taking Love's Lead
Edge of Living
Christmas Riches

Short story
The Second Act

Copyright

Cover Art by H.L Day
Edited by Alyson Roy - Royal Editing Services
Proofreading by Judy Zweifel at Judy's Proofreading
http://www.judysproofreading.com[1]
Eager For More © 2020 H.L Day

All Rights Reserved:
This literary work may not be reproduced or transmitted in any form or by any means including electronic or photographic reproduction, in whole or in part, without express written permission.

Eager For More is a work of fiction. Names, characters, places, and incidents either are the product of the author's imagination or are used fictitiously, and any resemblance to actual persons, living or dead, business establishments, events, or locales is entirely coincidental.

Warning
Intended for an 18+ audience. This book contains material that may be offensive to some and is intended for a mature,

---

1. http://www.judysproofreading.com/

adult audience. It contains graphic language, explicit sexual content, and adult situations.

THANKS

Huge thanks to my beta readers Barbara, Sherry, and Jill.

Chapter One

CAIN

"Have you seen Nick anywhere?"

The guy with the neatly trimmed moustache shrugged, dismissing Cain's question as if it were of no consequence, which to him it probably wasn't. He was the third person Cain had asked in as many minutes, and it was the third non-answer he'd received. Deciding not to waste any more time on him, Cain moved away, his gaze searching the busy room. The only reason he'd come to the party in the first place was in the hope of seeing Nick. He changed his tack, trying to spot the one person who should definitely know Nick's whereabouts. He finally found him over on the opposite side of the room, trying to chat up a tall, leggy blonde who was at least a foot taller than he was.

Cain smiled as he squeezed himself between groups of party guests to make his way over there. Theo had been his best friend since the age of eleven and was about as lucky in love as Cain was, which was to say not very lucky at all. If he'd thought Theo stood the slightest chance with the statuesque goddess, he might have felt bad about interrupting them. As it was, she excused herself about 0.8 seconds after Cain's arrival, as if he were the answer to all her prayers and she'd just been waiting for the opportunity to escape.

Theo rounded on him immediately, his blue eyes accusatory. "Dude, seriously. What the fuck! You remember that guy in the bar last week, the one that it took you over an hour to pluck up the courage to go and speak to? Did I come and interrupt you when you were in full flow? No, I didn't. Know why? Because. I. Am. Your. Friend. And friends don't do that to each other. I will now, though. Next time I'm going to be right in there, getting in your way. Just to pay you back."

He let his friend's rant run its course, doing his best to stop his lips from curling up into a smile at all the indignant attitude being aimed his way. Only when Theo seemed to run out of bluster did Cain finally speak. "You really thought you stood a chance with her?"

His friend tipped his head to the side, considering the notion for far longer than it deserved, his lips finally twitching. "Probably not. She's a supermodel, or whatever they're called these days. But a man can dream, right?" He raised his finger toward Cain's face, wagging it. "And you could have let me wallow in that dream for a bit longer without waking me up."

Cain held his hands up in mock surrender. "Point taken. I'll go and put myself on the naughty step for a few minutes." Something suddenly occurred to him. "What's a supermodel doing at your parents' party anyway?"

"Not sure. I think she knows Nick. He probably represented her on a case or something. Or..." Theo's eyes lit up with barely suppressed glee. "Maybe he's taking a walk down the straight parade. If he's dating her, do you think once they're married she'll introduce me to all her hot model friends?" His expression turned dreamy. "Just me and five... no, it's my fantasy, let's make it *six* hot, busty women in a hot tub. All of us squeezed together. We'd drink champagne and then one would reach across and..."

"Okay, enough!" Theo's description was a little too close for comfort for Cain to a scene that Evan, the studio boss, had already decided he was going to make at EagerBoyz. He wanted to extend their repertoire to doing more group scenes rather than just duos and threesomes. Only, there wouldn't be any hot, busty women in that one. Just four horny men, including Cain himself, according to Evan. He'd spent a while sounding Cain out about it and Cain had shrugged and said, "Sure. I'd be up for it." He'd figured it could be fun.

He hadn't quite gotten around to telling his best friend that he made porn though. There just hadn't seemed to be a good time. Besides, what if Theo told Nick? For brothers, they were strangely close. Probably something to do with there only being a three-year age gap between them, and there was no way Cain wanted Nick to find out the deep, dark secret he'd been keeping for over a year since he'd started filming with EagerBoyz.

Even the thought of Nick had Cain's heart missing a beat and his skin breaking out in goosebumps. Nicolas Hackett, lawyer extraordinaire, and the man who'd been causing Cain's heart to trip over itself ever since his hormones had kicked in at age fourteen. He'd followed him around like a lost sheep, the then seventeen-year-old treating Cain like another younger brother. And that was the problem, wasn't it? While Cain had lusted after Nick with all the teenage zeal that he could muster, Nick had either been oblivious, or had just ignored it. He'd been friendly but nothing more. He'd ruffled Cain's hair and called him squirt, included him in everything, and laughed at his jokes. But he hadn't treated him any differently than he had his own brother. Hadn't looked at him with anything beyond a benign fondness.

Not a lot had changed since then, except for Cain managing to be a little bit cooler about his crush of ten years. Oh, and the fact that he saw Nick a lot less. Which brought him back to his whole reason for seeking Theo out in the first place. "Where's Nick tonight?"

Theo gave the room a quick scan as if he expected to be able to point and say "there he is" like Cain hadn't spent the better part of an hour searching in vain for him. "Dunno. Probably still at work." His brow furrowed. "You told me you were over him." Of course Theo knew about Cain's crush on his brother. There was no way he couldn't have known given that Cain had metaphorically elbowed him out of the way whenever his brother was around. "I am." *He wasn't.* "I just haven't seen him, and given that this is your parents' party to celebrate your dad's birthday, I would have thought he'd be here. You know to support them with... stuff."

His friend gave another shrug, already looking bored with the conversation, his gaze sliding toward the staircase that led upstairs. "There's still a console set up in my old bedroom. Want to sneak off and get some gaming time in?" And there was Cain's other deep, dark secret, the one he kept from the porn world. That's how he and Theo had first met: bonding over a mutual love of gaming. It wasn't just that they played games. They really *played* games. Some people went on benders and drank too much. He and Theo, they pulled weekend-long game marathons, only stopping for food. Role-playing games were their first love. Not many people could say that they'd completed every single Final Fantasy game, but he and Theo could. They were also huge World of Warcraft fans, boasting a huge number of online friends and acquaintances in the gaming community.

Nothing compared to the burst of adrenaline when you were trying to complete a quest or level up your character to be a great warrior. Not even making porn. Although, gaming didn't quite bring Cain to orgasm so there were some points in porn's favor. He gave some consideration to Theo's offer, his hands already starting to twitch at the prospect of wrapping them around a game controller. But what about Nick? He made other parts of Cain twitch, parts that wouldn't do as they were told when Nick was around. It was quite the quandary. Hang around and wait for Nick on the off chance he might turn up or forget all about him and go and immerse himself in another world. He caved when Theo aimed a narrow-eyed stare in his direction, knowing a refusal would bring on Theo's version of the Spanish Inquisition as he postulated loudly why Cain was so keen to hang out with his parents.

THEO THREW THE GAME controller down in disgust as his orc avatar lay lifeless on the ground after being set upon by a horde of dragons. "Fucking flag. Never wanted it anyway. The winged bastards can have it." He reached for the bowl of popcorn, cramming a large handful in his mouth while proceeding to try and talk. "Isgt mnoow jpadchtht?"

Cain shook his head when all his attempts to decipher the strange new language came to naught. "What?"

"I said..." He chewed and swallowed methodically. "...is that a new jacket?"

Cain nodded. He'd worn it to try and impress Nick. Not that anything seemed to impress Nick. The man was as cool and collected as the proverbial cucumber. Friendly but distant. Amiable but largely absent. It was doubtful—even if he had bothered to turn up to the party—that Nick would have noticed what Cain was wearing. He had enough problems getting Nick to notice *him*. It was like Cain just blended in with the background. He was a good-looking guy with a body he'd worked hard on. It wasn't as if EagerBoyz would have hired him if not. They liked all their men to be as aesthetically pleasing as possible. But Nick still seemed to see the pimply teenager who'd followed him around all those years ago. Or at least that was Cain's theory. It wasn't as if he'd ever asked the man himself. Or ever would. Sometimes he wondered what he saw in Nick. The man had all the attributes of a straitlaced prude, but something about him got Cain going like no one else did. He'd always wanted to find out what else lay beneath that unruffled exterior.

Theo leaned forward, his hand delving into Cain's collar to pull the label out. "Ooh! Designer. Look at you. I need to get some hours at the restaurant if the tips are that good."

It took Cain a few seconds to work out what the restaurant where Cain was a trainee manager had to do with it. Right, of course. Porn money had paid for the jacket, but given that he hadn't told Theo about that, then his friend could only assume that it had come from the job he did know about. He either needed to come clean or be a bit more careful about parading around in clothes that showed off his rather more comfortable financial status. He earned twice as much for filming one scene as he did for a shift at the restaurant. The truth hovered on Cain's tongue before he pushed it back. Not tonight. Not when there was a huge party happening beneath their feet and a risk of Theo taking the news in his own inimitable dramatic style and announcing it to all and sundry. "I've... er... been doing some extra hours. Covering someone who's been off ill." He didn't like lying but it was either that or pick a very bad time to come clean.

Theo's brow wrinkled. "Have you? When?"

Cain fought to keep the color he could feel working its way up his neck from reaching his face. He grabbed the other controller. "Are we playing or what? Bet I stay alive longer than you this time."

His friend's brow arched. "Oh, like that is it. I can kick your ass. I've done it enough times over the years." He picked up his controller with a mutinous grin on his face, something else that Cain had borne witness to multiple times over the years. As it was, despite calling in reinforcements, they barely saw the damn flag, never mind managed to capture it over the next ninety minutes. They needed to go back to quests, at least then they might have something to show for the time spent on the game. Finally, they gave up, Theo leaning back against the bed as he polished the popcorn off.

Cain made himself comfortable, wondering where his stick-thin friend put all the food he consumed. Theo was much thinner than his brother. Jesus, there he went again thinking about Nick. It was like he had a one-track mind. Only now that he'd led himself back down that road, he couldn't stop, his brain comparing Nick's muscled physique to Theo's. Despite being a kick-ass lawyer, Nick still found time to go out and do a lot of physical stuff like rock climbing and mountain biking. Cain wiped his mouth in case a bit of drool had escaped. Whereas Theo's exercise usually consisted of the walk from the couch to the fridge. Cain didn't do outdoor pursuits either but he was a regular visitor to the gym, especially since he'd started appearing naked on camera. No one wanted subscribers commenting on their love handles.

Placing the empty bowl of popcorn on the floor, Theo gave him an inquisitive look. "You're coming to the wedding, right?"

Extensive searching of his memory banks left Cain clueless as to what his friend was talking about. "What wedding?" His question received an eye roll in response.

"Carol's wedding. The one you told her that she didn't have to waste an invitation for because you were definitely going. She's already put your name on a placemat and everything, so you've got to go."

Carol was Theo's cousin, and a good friend seeing as she was only a year older than the two of them and had hung out with them for numerous summer holidays. Cain knew she was getting married soon, but for the life of him he couldn't recall the conversation that Theo was talking about. "Was I drunk?"

He snorted. "Well, let's look at the evidence, shall we? Exhibit A—you'd had one glass of wine. Exhibit B—you're the biggest lightweight I know by far." He stretched his arms as wide as they would go for extra emphasis as he said the last two words. "So I'd say that it's odds on that yes, you were drunk." Theo sat back and crossed his arms, a smug expression on his face. "No further questions, your honor."

Cain opened his mouth to argue but didn't really have a leg to stand on, given that he really was a lightweight. The merest sniff of alcohol seemed to go to his head. That's why he hadn't touched a drop tonight. "Alright, mini Nick. You don't need to hammer it home. This wedding, when is it?"

"Weekend after next. Hotel room's already been booked for you. You just need to pay up and show up." A mischievous smile slid onto Theo's face. "Nick will be there."

Cain affected the most casual shrug he could muster and then ruined it completely with his next question. "Is he seeing anyone at the moment?" He ducked as a cushion came flying his way, the look of triumph on Theo's face only revealed once the cushion had landed without contact having been made.

"I knew you weren't over him."

Cain swallowed around a lump in his throat, sudden vulnerability threatening to suffocate him, even though he knew Theo didn't mean it maliciously. "Your brother's hot. And he has those suits." He paused at the grimace on his friend's face before deciding that he'd bloody brought the subject up, so he could suffer the consequences. "And I've seen him in court. He's all domineering and sexy. So, stop torturing me, is he seeing anyone?"

Theo shook his head. "Not that I know of." His expression turned sad. "You know he doesn't see you like that though, right?"

The lump in Cain's throat grew bigger. It was one thing knowing that, but it was another thing entirely to have someone else spell it out. And the sad thing was that it wasn't the first time. They revisited this conversation every few years, always with the same outcome. But what could he do? To everyone else it was a crush. But to him, it was more like unrequited love. If only there were some way he could get Nick to see him in a different light. To see the man he'd become rather than just his brother's friend. After ten years though, it was extremely unlikely. Nick might be single at the moment but he may as well be married or straight for all the good it did Cain.

"Sorry, man."

The sympathy did absolutely nothing to make him feel better either. He climbed to his feet. Now seemed like a really good time to leave before he got even more maudlin and ended up doing something stupid like crying.

Chapter Two

NICK

Nick stretched his long legs out in the back of the cab, massaging the back of his neck to try and ease the tight muscles there. He hadn't even been in court today, so he wasn't sure why he felt so exhausted. Although, he'd had wall-to-wall meetings in preparation for an upcoming case the following week, so that might have had something to do with it. He'd have liked nothing more than to go straight home, have a bath, and in the absence of a current boyfriend, a long, leisurely wank.

He reached for his phone as it vibrated, the FaceTime call filling up the screen. He pulled it up to the right height so he could be seen as he pressed the button to take the call, the familiar face of his friend, Bailey, flashing up on the screen, his lopsided grin and the color in his cheeks revealing that he'd started celebrating the weekend early. "Hey, Bailey."

"Heeeey! Where are you?"

"In the back of a cab."

"Come to the bar. There's a group of us here. It's the new one near—"

Nick interjected quickly. If he let him carry on, he'd know everything about the bar from its decor to the price of the drinks and what time it closed before he'd be able to get a word in edgewise. Bailey was a close friend, but boy could he talk. Especially when alcohol had already loosened his tongue. "I can't."

Bailey put the characteristic whine in his voice that usually had men falling at his feet to do his bidding. "Why not? I feel like I haven't seen you for ages."

Nick chuckled. "You saw me last weekend, so you can drop the guilt trip."

"That is ages. Why can't you come? Are you going home and being all boring?"

"No, it's my dad's birthday and my parents are having a party. I've got to at least go and show my face there."

Bailey stuck his lower lip out. "Come to the bar after the party. Your parents are in their fifties, they're not going to be partying until the early hours of the morning. Not unless they're a lot wilder than you are and if so, they're invited too."

"You know that face doesn't work on me." Bailey fluttered his eyelashes as well and Nick shook his head. It was alright for Bailey, his only job was being a social butterfly. People not only paid him to show his face at social events, but he had a sizeable trust fund as well. No doubt he was being paid tonight just for being photographed at the new bar and for throwing a couple of posts on Instagram about it. Therefore, he didn't really get the "being tired after work" thing. He pretended he did, but there wasn't really any comparison between a couple of hours at an event and a day buried in the legalities of the British judicial system.

They'd known each other for years, Bailey making a beeline for Nick when their paths had crossed at an awards ceremony. After a one-night stand, they'd been surprised to realize that despite coming from very different worlds, and being very different people, they got on well together. So from meaningless sex, a meaningful friendship, which was far more valuable, had been forged. And lord knows not everyone could put up with Bailey. He was too much for most people. Too talkative. Too loud. Too bright. Too Bailey. But Nick quite liked it—it meant he could fade into the background while Bailey held court, and he had to admit that their friendship got him some interesting invites to places where he wouldn't otherwise have dreamt of going, adding some much-needed color to his life at times. He was tired, but maybe a few drinks at a bar would be good. It would definitely be more exciting than his parents' party where the topic of conversation was likely to be the new conservatory they'd just had built. "Maybe, I'll come. I'll see. It depends how long I stay at the party for."

Bailey flashed him a bright smile. "I knew I could talk you into it. I'll text you the address. Oh, by the way, keep next Friday evening free. There's an event that you don't want to miss."

Nick slid lower in the seat, his interest piqued. "Oh, really. What's that?"

"EagerBoyz is having a party to celebrate their three-year anniversary."

Despite the fact that Bailey had said the name like it should mean something to him, it rang absolutely zero bells. "EagerBoyz? Sounds pretty tacky."

"Tacky!" Bailey's face came closer to the camera revealing his sparkly blue eyeshadow. "Darling, it is *not* tacky. It's art." Narrowing his eyes, probably at the lack of belief Nick knew was written all over his face, he tutted before elaborating. "I should have known you'd be oblivious to their fine body of work. Not kinky enough for you."

Nick stiffened at Bailey's comment, his eyes darting to the back of the cab driver's head, but the man didn't seem remotely interested in the conversation going on in the back of his cab. The word kinky sat like a leaden stone in Nick's gut. He could count the people who knew his secret on one hand, and sometimes he looked back and wondered how Bailey had ever gotten himself added to that list. The answer was simple: add a grueling day at work to too much tequila on a night out and the result was a loose-lipped Nick spilling secrets like an out-of-control volcano. To give Bailey his due, he hadn't laughed, he hadn't mocked him, he'd just asked a few pertinent questions and then as far as Nick knew, he'd kept his secret ever since. "You've lost me."

Bailey rolled his eyes. "EagerBoyz is a porn studio. All the stars are going to be attending the party. The very yummy Angel, who's like the pioneer of the company, the trailblazer who laid the foundations for everyone else to follow. You should check his scenes out; he has so many that I always tell everyone that there's a little something for everyone. There's Blaze who has a cock to die for. And to be honest"—he winked—"unless you're as skilled as I am, death is a distinct possibility given its size. I'm so looking forward to meeting him. Do you think he'd show me if I asked nicely? I guess it never hurts to ask. I hate to waste an opportunity. Who else is there? Oh, there's some lovely scrumptious newbies like Leo and Tyler. Oh, and Cain. I can't forget Cain. He's such a hunk. I think he probably has the best body out of the lot of them. Very fuckable. Always looks a little sad though. Like he'd rather have a hug than a fuck."

The familiar name of Cain caused a jolt in Nick's chest until he reminded himself that there were plenty of people with that name in the world. The idea of his brother's friend making porn was just too bizarre to even contemplate. He'd never seen him with a boyfriend for longer than two minutes, never mind performing on camera for money. Realizing that Bailey was still working his way through the entire roster of porn stars, he made an effort to tune back in. Knowing Bailey there'd be a test at the end.

"...gorgeous freckles absolutely all over his body. He left though, so I doubt he'll be at the party. I wonder what he's doing now. I might have to do a little googling and see if I can track him down. Although, I think he's exclusively a bottom and you know what they say about two bottoms getting together, so it probably wouldn't work. He'll have to be the one that got away."

"Bailey."

"I'm sure I must have missed someone."

"Bailey."

The second repetition of his name finally got his attention. "What, darling?"

"I have to go. I've just reached my parents' house."

He sighed, his sparkly blue eyelids lowering as he did so. "You're not going to make the bar tonight, are you?"

Nick did a quick inventory. Even the thought of going inside the house and socializing at his parents' party seemed exhausting. "Probably not."

"But you'll come next Friday for the wall-to-wall eye candy? I'm hoping they'll be oiled up. Imagine that, and if they're not, I can offer to do it for them. I'll even..."

Laughing, Nick cut him off again. "I really do have to go. I'll see you on Friday. I'll even bring the oil." He blew him a kiss before ending the call, wishing that some of Bailey's boundless energy could have soaked into him. He eyed the front door, reminding himself that he was on his way to a party, not an execution. It wouldn't be as interesting as Friday's party was apparently going to be, given that there weren't going to be any porn stars here, but he'd make do.

HE'D BARELY SET FOOT in the door before someone barreled straight into him. Nick automatically put his hand out to steady the guy, his fingers meeting firm muscle through a thin shirt covered by a leather jacket. For a moment, he enjoyed the sensation before lifting his head to see the guy's face. All lustful thoughts disappeared in a flash at the sight of his brother's best friend. He dropped his hand so fast his fingers may as well have been on fire. When had Cain gotten so buff? He could have sworn that all that muscle had come out of nowhere. Was it just because he couldn't recall ever having seen him in a shirt before? Cain was more of a jeans and hoodie guy.

Okay, so not all lustful thoughts went away. He certainly buried them, though. Of all the people to start thinking about in that way, Cain wasn't it for a multitude of reasons. Like the flak he'd get from his brother if he so much as put a foot out of line. The two of them were just about joined at the hip. If it wasn't for the fact that his brother was straight, he'd have had his suspicions about what the two of them really got up to behind closed doors. Then, of course, there was the fact that for the longest period of time Cain had seemed to have some sort of weird hero worship fixation on him. He shook his head to clear it, using the jolt to make his tongue work. "Hey, sorry, squirt." Squirt was what Nick had always called Cain since he was a teenager. It had just stuck.

"You still calling me that?"

Nick grinned. "Course I am. You'll always be squirt to me."

Cain's sigh was long and weary. It wasn't like him at all. Nick grabbed his arm, again noting the muscle bunching under his fingertips, and pulled him over to one side away from the door. "Hey, you alright?"

"Do you care?"

Okay, this definitely wasn't the happy-go-lucky guy Nick was used to seeing. What was going on with him? "Of course I do."

"Why?"

There was something almost confrontational in both Cain's tone and the way he was staring at Nick. Had he done something to piss him off? Unlikely, given that it had to have been at least a couple of months since they'd last bumped into each other, and that had been at most a five-minute conversation. From what Nick could recall, it hadn't featured anything more controversial than questions about each other's work and the usual "how are you doing?" chit-chat. "Because you're my brother's friend and I've known you for years." Cain's expression darkened even more, leaving Nick with no idea what was going on. He cast around for a possible explanation, voicing the first one that came to mind. "Did you and Theo have an argument?"

A small sliver of humor broke through Cain's otherwise stony expression. "When have we ever argued?"

It was a good point. Even when one of them tried to get annoyed with the other, it usually lasted all of five seconds. Nick smiled, trying to lighten the mood a little. "I don't know, you geeks seem to have your own set of rules that the rest of us just don't get."

It did the complete opposite of what Nick had intended, Cain's gaze darting towards the door as if he couldn't wait to get away. Sure enough, his next words confirmed it. "I have to go. I'm late for... something."

Frowning, Nick stepped out of the way. "Sure. I didn't mean to keep you from something. Just wanted to say hello."

Cain managed a smile, but it didn't reach his eyes and Nick was again left wondering what he'd missed. Should he push a bit more? Cain was, after all, almost family. Before he could, though, Cain had already backed off a couple of steps. "Well, yeah, hello. See you around, I guess."

Nick barely had time to nod before Cain was already gone, disappearing through the door he'd been on his way out of prior to Nick's interception. That had been a strange little interlude. Something was definitely going on with Cain. If it had nothing to do with Theo, then it was something else. None of his business though, he guessed. He shrugged the encounter off and went to find his parents and an alcoholic drink. Not necessarily in that order.

IT WAS PAST ELEVEN by the time Nick got home. He'd had to field two more phone calls from Bailey, who had been determined to try and get him to join him at the bar. He had no idea why. It wasn't as if Bailey wasn't surrounded by his usual hangers-on. Maybe that was it. Nick hung out with Bailey because he liked him despite his little foibles, of which there were many. Not because he wanted to get free drinks or access to VIP areas out of him. He definitely couldn't say that about most of the people who regularly accompanied Bailey on nights out. Some of them were after as many freebies as they could get their hands on, while others were aspiring actors or models, more interested in appearing in the limelight. They'd never discussed it but Bailey wasn't a fool, so he must have been aware that the majority of them would have dropped him the moment he no longer proved useful to them. So Nick guessed that he was the exception. He got nothing from Bailey except friendship.

The last time Bailey had called he'd barely been coherent, so it had been all too easy to turn him down. Drunk Bailey was an even bigger nightmare than a sober one. The last time that had happened he'd tried to convince Nick that as all things retro were in vogue, they should go to bed together again and reignite their one-night stand of many years ago. Nick had almost had to throw him at the nearest available bartender to get him to drop that idea.

He smiled at the memory as he dropped his wallet and keys and on the table. It was too late for the bath he'd been craving earlier, so he settled for a shower instead, taking a long, leisurely one as a compromise. His hands roamed down over his abdomen, palming his cock and remembering his earlier urge to have a wank. Except the limp organ seemed to be having none of it. It was obviously just as tired as he was.

Turning the shower off, Nick wrapped himself in a towel and padded over to the chest of drawers in his bedroom, intending to get something out to sleep in. His fingers paused on the handle of the top drawer, trailing slowly downward almost of their own accord until he reached the bottom one. He swallowed, his chest tightening and his throat thickening. He could feel the familiar heat invading his cheeks as well, even though he knew he was alone. Every time, it was the same. The same battle to avoid temptation, to simply step away and do something else. To be someone else. And every time he lost.

He gripped the drawer and pulled it open, staring at the fluffy blue towel that he always positioned carefully over the top of the drawer's contents. Just in case he ever had any overnight guests who might go snooping—or a burglar. The theory was that they'd open the drawer and decide that it contained nothing more interesting than towels and close it again without going any further. As far as he knew the theory had never been tested, given he'd had zero burglars and far too few overnight guests.

His fingers grazed the blue towel, slowly peeling the corner away to reveal what lay underneath. He had the same reaction he always did, his breath catching in his throat and his heart kicking into overdrive as he stared at the sea of lace and silk in a multitude of colors. Yes, Nicholas Hackett, fearless lawyer in the courtroom, got off on wearing women's underwear in the privacy of his own home. He ran his fingers through the drawer like it was a beach of sand. Only sand wouldn't cause the same effect that the mixture of fabrics had on him. His breathing picked up, his skin broke out in goosebumps, and as for his cock, the same cock that had been so unresponsive in the shower... well, it was suddenly incredibly interested. And still he fought it. He tried to tell himself that any second now he would remove his hand from the drawer, close it, and go to bed.

Bailey kept trying to tell him that there was nothing wrong with having certain tastes. But there had to be, right? God knows the couple of ex-boyfriends he'd been brave enough to tell in the past hadn't agreed. It had taken guts to work up to that point, and at least a year of them having been together. And for what? Boyfriend number one had straight-out called him a pervert and they'd broken up less than a month later. And as for boyfriend number two, things had started better, with grudging acceptance, but then their relationship had changed in unforeseen ways. Where he'd been happy enough for Nick to top before the reveal, he hadn't been able to get his head around the fact that Nick wanted to wear women's underwear and still top.

He'd seemed to think that once Nick put the underwear on, he'd want to take on a submissive role and get fucked instead. They'd even tried it, but it had left a distinctly bitter taste in Nick's mouth. He didn't want to get called "bitch" and roleplay someone pulling his hair and treating him like a whore. That's not what it was about at all. He wanted to do everything he usually did, only with the added stimulation of his cock being encased in lace or silk.

No one understood.

Except for maybe Bailey. But then Bailey didn't give a fuck what anyone thought, about anything. He delighted in flaunting his sexuality to all and sundry, almost seeming to feed on people's shock like some sort of emotional vampire. And he wore whatever the fuck he wanted to as well, including makeup and high heels. Bailey was lucky though. He just needed to party and look fabulous; he didn't need to go into court and put criminals behind bars. Nobody was going to take Nick seriously if they knew that behind closed doors, he needed to wear skimpy panties in order to feel sexually fulfilled. He didn't know what he'd do if the secret ever got out. Go into hiding probably. He definitely didn't think he'd ever be able to show his face in a courtroom again. The thought almost had him closing the drawer. Almost.

His fingers hovered over a number of choices before settling on a pair of pink satin panties. Still fighting against a healthy dose of self-recrimination, he pulled them out. From there on in, there was no more debate as he pulled the panties up over his thighs, every brush of the material over his bare skin igniting the flames within until by the time he settled them over his groin, his cock was straining at the front.

He walked over to the full-length mirror in the corner of the room, barely able to recognize the man with the flushed cheeks and glazed expression that stared back at him. He turned from one side to the other admiring the way the flimsy fabric stretched tight over his ass. It looked almost as good as it felt, his cock throbbing and his erection now so stiff that the head of his cock peeped over the waistband of the underwear. He made himself wait a whole minute, trying to force himself to breathe evenly and stretch out the delicious anticipation as long as he could. When he couldn't wait any longer, he spat on his palm before shoving his hand down the front of the panties and grasping hold of his cock.

He watched himself in the mirror as he stroked his cock, the sight ramping up the pleasure that little bit more. Each stroke made the silky fabric pull tight against his balls, an exquisite slide of pure ecstasy. Then, all too soon, he was coming, his cock jerking in his hand and tiny pearls of cum hitting the mirror, as well as the pink satin. He slumped against the mirror, panting and marveling as he always did, how the act of indulging himself in this way could change his orgasm from something functional to something awe inspiring.

He had a few seconds of bliss, a few precious seconds where everything seemed right with the world, and then the fingers of shame started to insert themselves into Nick's brain again, reminding him that he was a pervert who was always going to be alone.

Chapter Three

CAIN

Cain had acknowledged a hard truth back at Theo's parents' house when he'd bumped into Nick. Nick was never going to be interested in him. Nick was never going to see him any differently and it shouldn't have taken him ten years to realize that. What had it taken to reach that truth? Three things in rapid succession. The way Nick had snatched his hand away from Cain as if he might be contagious once he'd recognized who he had his hands on. His persistence in calling him squirt, and then the icing on the cake, the way the suave lawyer had blithely used the word geek to describe Cain.

He should be thanking Nick, really. It was like waking up from a coma he'd been trapped in for several years and getting the chance to live again. So for once, he hadn't stayed at the party soaking up every crumb of attention he could get, he'd gotten the hell out of there. Since then he'd taken a long, hard look at his life and he'd decided a few things.

He worked in a porn studio surrounded by hot, horny men. All he needed to do was find one to provide the necessary distraction needed off camera. And maybe if he played his cards right, it might lead to more. Just because they made porn didn't mean they weren't boyfriend material.

His first port of call had been Angel. After filming a scene with him, he'd made it perfectly clear that he was up for more.

How had Angel responded? He'd avoided Cain altogether, choosing to stay behind and talk to Evan rather than hit the showers. It had been a bit of a kick in the teeth if Cain was honest. But then, Angel was renowned for being difficult. Hot as fuck and sexy as sin. But difficult. He did his own thing and rarely socialized with the rest of them, so Cain had tried not to take it too personally.

Cain had filmed with Blaze that afternoon, his co-star putting his huge cock to good use. So much so that standing at the bar waiting for drinks, the twinge in Cain's ass kept reminding him of how he'd spent the last few hours. It was one thing to bottom for a well-endowed guy in real life, but having to do it for much longer in every conceivable position really made your eyes water. He cast a glance back over his shoulder to where Blaze was seated in a booth with a few of the other EagerBoyz stars, his eyes focusing on Blaze for longer than they needed to. He was hot—obviously. And he was a lot friendlier than Angel was. Mind, that didn't mean a lot. Ninety-nine percent of the population were friendlier than Angel. Should he make a move on him? Just because he'd been turned down once didn't mean it would happen again. Maybe he'd play it by ear. He needed something to stop him from thinking about Nick. He stopped himself as soon as the name popped into his head. He wasn't even going to think about him.

The concentration Cain needed to carry the tray of drinks across the crowded bar wasn't helped by the continual catcalls aimed in his direction. The problem with collecting a group of porn stars together was that they weren't just rowdy, everything had to have a double meaning like they were back in the seventies auditioning for a part in a *"Carry on"* movie.

"Hey, Blaze. He can still walk. What's with that? Has your dick shrunk?"

"Cain, I've heard you're good at not spilling any liquids. It better be true. I want my beer in one piece. Don't use your mouth, though."

They all laughed hysterically as if they thought they were stand-up comedians and their jokes had never been heard before.

Reaching the table, Cain placed the tray carefully on its surface, hands shooting out from every direction to grab their drinks. He eased himself back into the seat next to Blaze, glad that no one had taken it while he was at the bar. He clinked his bottle against Blaze's and gave himself the luxury of admiring his companion. Blaze was his studio name of course, not his real name, but they tended to stick to the same names outside the studio. Actually, that was more at Evan's insistence. He didn't have many rules but that was one of them. Apparently, there'd been way too many incidents where the wrong name had slipped out during filming, making editing a nightmare.

For most of them, it probably got confusing. Cain had definitely witnessed a few incidents where someone had called another guy's name, only for the other person to completely ignore them until they remembered that the name belonged to them. For him, it was easy: he'd kept the same name. It hadn't been intentional. What person in their right mind chose to keep the same name when they started making porn? But tasked with coming up with an alternative he was comfortable with, he'd drawn a big, fat blank. They were either too cheesy, like Python or Phoenix, or sounded way too normal like Brian or Keith. In the end Evan had pointed out that Cain would work, and he'd gone with it. So he was Cain in real life *and* on-screen, and it was too late to change it even if he wanted to. Which to be honest, he wasn't that bothered about it. Most of his friends were straight, or just weren't that into watching gay porn.

He studied Blaze surreptitiously from beneath his lashes. Blaze was gorgeous, all ebony muscled skin and long, dark hair. Despite the soreness of his ass, Cain's cock gave an interested twitch.

Catching his scrutiny, Blaze smiled, his eyes lidding seductively. "What are you thinking about?"

Cain mentally took a deep breath. This was the bit he usually screwed up. When he'd joined the EagerBoyz studio, he'd expected to find a whole stable of horny, oversexed men. They were, but it seemed *only* for sex. And when it came down to it, yes, he wanted sex, but he wanted a bit more than that. He wanted sex to lead to some sort of connection, maybe even a relationship. But so far, after a year of working there, it had led to nothing more than a repeat outside the studio of what they'd already done inside. He remained optimistic though. And now that he wasn't going to be thinking about Nick anymore, and he wasn't going to be comparing everyone to a tall blond in a perfectly tailored charcoal suit, it should be a hell of a lot easier.

Flirting, right? He could do that. After all, Blaze had asked him what he was thinking about. He wasn't going to get a better opening than that. He cleared his throat, aiming for an edge of sexy huskiness that he usually reserved for the camera. "I was thinking about this afternoon. Our scene. How much I enjoyed it and…" He leaned forward into Blaze's space, his fingers nudging his thigh. "…how I'd like to do it again, but maybe have dinner first this time." Cain gave himself a metaphorical high five. That was perfect. Flirty but making it perfectly clear he wasn't just after a quick fuck.

Blaze's lips curled up into an amused smile. "Dinner?" He contemplated it for a moment as if it were an alien concept. "I guess I gotta eat. So I suppose I could do dinner."

"Hey, Cain. You filmed with Ryker yet?"

Cain cursed the interruption from across the table when things were just starting to fall into place, but politely turned his head in the direction of the question-asker. "No, not yet. I think Evan said it's on the schedule for next month. You know what he's like though, he changes his mind all the time. Why you asking?"

Tyler winked. "We were discussing who gives the best blow jobs. We got it down to being between you and Ryker, so we figured we'd get your take on it. Guess it'll be a battle of the blow jobs when you two finally film together."

The expected reaction was to either say something dirty, or laugh like a hyena. Only, Cain couldn't seem to muster either tonight. He wasn't in the mood for mindless jibes. Not when he was trying to sort out a candlelit dinner with the man who'd spent all afternoon fucking him, in order to find out more about him than just his dick size and the way he moaned when he came. He managed a shrug, Blaze rescuing him by leaning over to whisper in his ear. "Want to lose these drunken idiots for a while?"

Did he ever.

They left the table amid a cacophony of wolf whistles and insinuations, Blaze dragging him over to an empty booth in the corner that was far enough away from the EagerBoyz group that they couldn't hear them anymore. Cain sank into the seat, glad for the opportunity for a bit of peace and quiet, as well as some time alone with Blaze. "Thanks. They're a bit much today."

"They're just giddy because of that group scene Evan's announced he's going to film. They're all desperate to get picked so they can have a few days filming in Spain all expenses paid. You're wanting to go, right?"

Cain shrugged. Evan had mentioned it to him, but he suspected Evan had sounded everyone out about it. "When is it?" He couldn't see that filming in Spain was that much different to filming in London. It wasn't like they'd have that much time outside filming to sightsee. He supposed it would be warmer, which was always a bonus. But apart from that he could take it or leave it. A weekend would mean having to organize time away from working at the restaurant, which would also mean having to come up with an excuse other than that he was going to be making porn.

"End of February."

"Depends if it clashes with Comic Con." The words were out before Cain could stop them. He could have kicked himself.

Blaze's forehead furrowed, his fingers tapping on the table. "Comic what?"

Ironic really, that Cain would have given anything now for a distraction. Except it was just him and Blaze, so there wasn't going to be any interruption, leaving him with no other option but to answer the question. "It's a... convention thing that happens every year." He picked at the label on his beer bottle, praying that Blaze would let it drop.

"What sort of convention?" Blaze pulled his phone out of his pocket and tapped a few buttons. "What did you call it? Comic what?"

"Con... it's—"

Blaze laughed out loud, his eyes fixed on whatever had come up on his phone. "You're into that. Oh my God! Look at the pictures." He turned the phone around, but not for long enough for Cain to be able to see what was apparently so hilarious. "Do you dress up?"

"I..." What was he supposed to say to that? He had in the past. It was all part of the fun. World of Warcraft gave them some great scope for costume choices. He and Theo usually liked to match, so over the years they'd done everything from trolls to elves. Blaze was still staring at him expectantly, waiting for an answer. Cain ducked his head, heat flooding his cheeks and mumbled, "Not every year."

It didn't take him long to realize that he'd just made it ten times worse by revealing that it wasn't just a one-off thing, but that he was a regular. A quick glance Blaze's way revealed that he was still swiping through photos, the expression on his face akin to someone having found a quaint museum full of curiosities. Cain's chance of a date crumbled into dust in front of him. Actually, did he even want one with someone who mocked other people just because they had different tastes? He stood up from the table. "I need to take a piss."

Blaze lifted his head for a few seconds. "Sure, man. Whatever. Oh jeez! This guy's painted himself green. What an idiot. Fancy not only being seen in public like that but letting yourself get photographed. What's with these people? I might go to this thing just for a laugh."

Cain walked away, not needing to hear any more. He took his time in the bathroom, spending far more time washing his hands than he needed to. When he came out the booth was empty and Blaze was nowhere to be seen. He couldn't decide whether it was a shame or an absolute fucking godsend. One thing was for sure, it wouldn't be long before the rest of the EagerBoyz found out that in his spare time he liked to dress up. Fan-fucking-tastic. They were going to have a field day mocking him for this one. The geek jokes would be never-ending. There was a reason he'd kept it on the down low.

Chapter Four

NICK

Bailey strutted up and down in front of the mirror, admiring himself from different angles. "I'm not sure."

Nick sighed, his patience starting to wear thin. This was the fourth outfit Bailey had tried on. "It's just a party."

His friend rounded on him, the hazel eyes ringed by eyeliner flashing a warning just before the rant started. "Just a party! This is not *just* a party. *This* is where the right outfit will get me my pick of hot, hunky porn stars wanting to do unspeakable things to me. Maybe... I'll even get to pick more than one." He gave a pronounced shudder. "Oh, just think about it. A porn star orgy. How much fun would that be?"

The grimace Nick pulled in response said it all. He could think of nothing worse. Oh, don't get him wrong, he was intrigued to meet a room full of porn stars and find out what they were like, and if one took his fancy, then he wasn't exactly averse to a quickie. After all, things had been a little sparse on that front lately. But an orgy? No, thanks. Not his style. "Maybe you should just turn up naked, then, if that's what you're after."

Bailey shot him a dirty look. "Darling, I love you, but you are completely clueless. These are porn stars. They're surrounded by naked flesh day after day. I need to stand out, not fade into the background." His gaze raked over Nick. "You might not worry about your outfit, but some of us are a bit more discerning." He paused, focusing on Nick's crotch, one eyebrow lifting. "Are you...?"

"No!" Nick couldn't stop the heat from flooding to his cheeks. "I've told you before that it's just when I'm at home and even then, not all the time. Just, you know, when I need it." Sailing perilously close to rambling, he stopped talking.

Unfortunately, it didn't stop Bailey from staring at him, his head tilted to the side as he considered whatever it was that he was considering. "Shame! I love the idea of you going into court all businesslike and officious"—his mouth turned up wickedly at the corners—"and underneath your suit is a tantalizing glimpse of—"

"Stop!" Nick climbed off the bed before Bailey could say more. Even the mention of such a scenario had parts of him tingling that he really didn't need to be doing so, particularly at the start of the evening. Looking to distract Bailey, he walked over to his wardrobe, pulling the first thing he saw off a hanger. "What about this?" *This* turned out to be a red silk waistcoat. Not the best thing to be handling when he wanted to forget about the other conversation, given that it reminded him of the pair of panties he'd bought online from... no, not going there. Not now. He shoved it into Bailey's arms, needing the touch of the fabric somewhere other than on his skin in case his cock got the wrong idea.

Bailey held it up to the light, his nose wrinkling. "Where is it that you think we're going, darling... a formal dinner?" His eyes suddenly lit up. "Unless..." He quickly stripped off what he'd been wearing on his top half, not bothering to put a shirt on before donning the waistcoat. It left his muscular arms bare as well as a fair portion of his chest on display where the waistcoat dipped before the buttons started. He returned to the mirror, resuming his scrutiny of all angles. "Hmm... who knew you could actually have a good eye for anything to do with fashion." His gaze skated down over the plain trousers and shirt that Nick had decided were entirely appropriate for a party. "Not me, that's for sure."

The best policy was to ignore the backhanded compliment/jibe. Besides, Nick could hardly take credit for it really when it had just been pure dumb luck. He checked his watch. They'd been in Bailey's bedroom for an hour. At this rate, the party would be over before they got there. "Are we ready to go, then?" A sigh escaped from his lips as Bailey shook his head and returned to evaluating himself in the mirror. That lasted for at least a minute before Bailey crossed back over to the wardrobe and started rummaging through it.

When his blond head finally appeared back out of it, he was holding a pair of red high heels in one hand. "Trousers are okay but now the shoes don't match." Toeing off what he'd been wearing, he swapped them for the heels, leaning on Nick's shoulder for support as he threatened to overbalance. Nick held himself still, counting to ten in his head. "*Now*, are you ready?"

Bailey stepped back, the heels bringing him up to the same height as Nick, meaning that Nick couldn't fail to miss the withering look that he was on the receiving end of. Bailey picked up a tissue, removing the pink lipstick he'd been wearing and slowly and carefully replacing it with a red that matched the shoes and the waistcoat. Then he was back to the mirror, mussing his blond hair until he'd teased it to a deliberately disarrayed perfection. Bailey scrutinized his reflection one more time. "I look hot, right?"

"Very hot." Nick didn't need to lie. Bailey did look hot.

It wasn't enough for Bailey, though. He tipped his chin up. "Hot enough to have porn stars fighting over me?"

A smile hovered on Nick's lips despite his impatience to get going. "Definitely."

His friend let loose a blinding smile. "Then I'm ready. Let's go."

Nick followed him to the door, relieved beyond belief that they were finally leaving. He'd begun to think that he'd have to spend the entire night in Bailey's bedroom, and not in a good way. Watching someone try on every item of clothing they owned wasn't his idea of a good time. He was ready for a drink and a bit of eye candy. He grabbed Bailey's arm as they approached the bedroom door. "Don't you need a jacket or something?"

The look he got in response to his question was positively scathing. "Honestly, have I taught you nothing over the years?" Bailey waved his hands in a dramatic fashion over the length of his body. "We've just agreed that I look fabulous. Why would I even *think* about covering that amount of fabulosity up with a coat?"

Nick stifled a smile at the outrage on Bailey's face. It was as if he'd suggested putting a wetsuit on, or borrowing his grand-dad's trench coat. "No idea."

Bailey huffed as he made his way downstairs, Nick almost walking into him as he suddenly stopped and whirled around. "And once we get there, make sure it doesn't come across like we're together."

"How?"

"I don't know. You're the one that's meant to have all the brains out of the two of us. Make it subtle but clear."

The urge to snap a salute was strong but somehow Nick managed to resist it. Bailey was the only person who got away with bossing him around. Maybe that was why he liked hanging out with him. It was somewhat relaxing to be told what to do rather than have to think for himself.

THE PARTY WAS BEING held in a nightclub, and Bailey approached the doorman, flashing a smile first, and then his invitation. The invitation barely got a glance, the man more interested in looking Bailey over, his gaze lingering for a long time on Bailey's bare shoulders. Nick shook his head wearily. It was like watching a spider weave its web and then watching all the flies happily surrender. Then again, he couldn't really talk. It might have been a few years back, but at one point in time he'd been one of those flies.

Bailey shot him a narrow-eyed look. "What?" When Nick didn't say anything, his expression changed to one of amusement. "It doesn't hurt to flirt, you know. You should try it someday. You never know, you might like it."

Whatever Nick might have said in response was pushed out of his head as they stepped into the room where the party was being held. He stared around it in astonishment. "Holy fuck!"

Nodding sagely, Bailey grinned at him. "I know, right. How cool is this?"

Cool was most definitely not the word that Nick would have used. He thought he'd prepared himself for most things before attending the party, but never in his wildest imagination could he have foreseen the decor. The walls were covered in huge, and huge was not an exaggeration, stills from what he could only assume, given their pornographic content, were from the EagerBoyz films. To his right was a larger-than-life technicolor print of a naked muscular man lying on a bed, his hand wrapped around his stiff cock while his face demonstrated a look of ecstasy, giving the impression he was no more than a few seconds away from coming.

Nick looked away, only to be confronted by the picture on his left, which was worse... or better depending on your viewpoint as it contained a tangle of limbs from two men in the middle of a fucking scene. Nick squinted at the picture. No, not two men, three men, unless one of the men had four arms. "Jesus."

Bailey grabbed his arm, pulling him away from the doorway and over to a bar. "You've gone very religious tonight, darling." A conversation with the barman later, he pushed a drink into Nick's hand. "Here. Drink this. You could do with loosening up a bit. You're gawping. It's like you've never seen a naked man before."

Nick lifted a hand, waving it weakly in the direction of the nearest picture—one that was a close-up of a blow job. "They're so big."

Bailey tipped his head to one side, evaluating the picture. "Not really. That's Tyler. He's about average, really. He—"

"Not the... cock. The picture. I didn't expect them."

"Oh, I see. What did you think they'd decorate the place with? They're a porn company celebrating their anniversary of making porn. Vases of flowers and cute animals wouldn't really cut it. Speaking of celebrating, here comes Evan now."

Nick didn't have a clue who Evan was as he watched Bailey throw himself whole-heartedly into air kisses and enthusing about how good the place looked. He concentrated on sipping the drink Bailey had gotten for him, wondering whether it was wise to be starting the evening with whisky. His thoughts soon turned to trying to work out who Evan was. Although good-looking, he seemed a little too old and a little too unkempt with his shaggy blond hair to be one of the models.

Finally seeming to clue into his ignorance, Bailey grabbed his arm and pulled him closer. "This is my friend, Nick. Excuse him for standing around with his mouth open. I think he's a little overwhelmed with all the beauty on display. Nick, this is Evan. He owns EagerBoyz. He's the man behind the magic, you might say."

Nick shook Evan's hand while trying to work out what he was supposed to say. In the end he settled for congratulating him and muttering something about what a fun day job Evan must have, and then thankfully Evan and Bailey went back to whatever it is that they were talking about, giving Nick a chance to take stock beyond the artwork on the walls.

Rather than being late, they seemed to have gotten there fairly early, the room only just starting to fill up as more guests arrived, none of them seeming to have the same reaction to the photos on the wall that Nick had. In fact, there were quite a few people strolling around the room, with drinks in hand, and stopping to discuss each picture as if they were in the National Gallery.

It was easy to spot the porn stars in the room for two reasons. They were all shirtless and each and every one had a rapidly growing cluster of people around them. A little more used to his surroundings now, either that or the whisky had kicked in, Nick let his gaze peruse the naked torsos of some of the stars. They were all extremely fit and muscular, but then he supposed that was to be expected. They weren't oiled up though; Bailey would be disappointed. Yet, for some reason they did absolutely nothing for him. Perhaps he just didn't want to be a part of the crowd already drooling over them, or maybe it was because the pictures on the wall took away any air of mystery that there might have been. They may as well have been half-naked women for all the interest they sparked in Nick's groin.

He finished the whisky, heading back over to the bar to place the empty glass down. As he did, the muscular back of another porn star caught his eye. He traced the taut back muscles down to a trim waist and a delectable ass encased in tight black trousers. Okay, it would seem that he wasn't immune to *all* of the porn stars. This one definitely deserved a second *and* a third look, his cock reacting accordingly.

He had a little group of hangers-on, just like the rest, one woman reaching out to wrap her hand around his biceps before pretending to swoon. Nick rolled his eyes. She may as well have lain down on the ground, spread her legs and offered herself up as tribute. Nick moved slightly over to one side, hoping to be able to catch a glimpse of the model's face, but there were too many people blocking his view.

Then his view was completely blocked as Bailey moved to stand in front of him, Evan having moved over to another group, presumably to mingle. Another whisky was pushed into his hands and Nick dutifully drank some more as Bailey stared at him expectantly. "Evan is such a sweetie, and would you believe that he never touches any of his models?"

Nick could believe it. It was called professionalism and having restraint, but as Bailey wasn't big on the concept of restraint in any shape or form, he didn't bother to try and explain it to him. It would be like trying to explain the taste and texture of meat to a vegan.

Bailey was still talking. "So I'm going to go and mingle and introduce myself to as many of these hunks as I can. Try not to just stand in a corner and pout, would you, darling. I'm guessing we'll probably end up leaving separately, because"—he winked—"I have no intention of going home on my own, but feel free to call for my driver to come and pick you up when you're ready to leave. You've got his number in your phone, haven't you? Have fun!"

It wasn't until Bailey turned away that Nick realized he wasn't joking and that he had every intention of the two of them parting ways. He lunged forward, grabbing his friend by the arm, and spinning him around to face him. "Hang on! You can't just leave me. I don't know any of these people. You could at least introduce me to some of them first."

Bailey stared at him owlishly, amusement sparkling in his hazel eyes. "I only know Evan and I already introduced you to him." He patted Nick's arm in what was meant to be a consoling fashion. "You'll do fine. Just try not to come across as having too much of a stick up your ass. Less lawyer and more..."

His nose wrinkled as he considered what word he could use. "...I don't know, something that has a bit more fun."

He blew a kiss and then he was gone, disappearing into the crowd. Why had Bailey brought him along if he had no intention of spending any time with him? He may as well have come on his own. It wasn't typical behavior from Bailey, but then they'd never been in the situation before where Bailey was surrounded by wall-to-wall naked flesh. It must have gone to his head and erased any traces of the usual loyalty he displayed.

Nick took another sip of whisky while he contemplated his options. He could go home and leave Bailey to it, but that seemed a shame when he'd come all this way. It would mean he'd endured the trial of many outfits back in Bailey's bedroom for nothing. Or he could, as Bailey had put it, "lose the stick in his ass" and try and enjoy himself. His gaze unwittingly moved back to the man he'd been admiring before. Why not? What was the worst that could happen? He could get blown off. So what? It wouldn't be the first time in his life. Nobody else in the room seemed to care that they were virtually throwing themselves at porn stars in an effort to be another notch on their bedpost. What was the saying, if you can't beat them, join them? It wasn't as if he was ever going to see any of the people in this room again, with the exception of Bailey, after tonight.

The group had moved, so it took a while for Nick to locate the man he was searching for. He was facing him this time, but his view was still obstructed, so Nick started his perusal with the bits he could see, which was mostly below the waist. He quickly skimmed over the feet and lower legs, those parts of the anatomy holding little interest. He lingered for slightly longer on the muscular thighs before pausing at the view that the tight trousers afforded him of the guy's crotch. *Nice package.* Very nice indeed. The man who'd been standing in the way moved aside allowing Nick to continue his scrutiny. The man's chest was even nicer. He must spend a lot of time in the gym to have developed abdominal muscles and pectoral muscles like that, not to mention the beefy arms. Yeah, Nick was definitely interested. Interested enough to risk the stinging rejection that was likely to come his way when he made a move. Nothing ventured, nothing gained. Christ! He was full of clichés tonight. He'd have to try and make sure that his chat-up speech wasn't littered with them.

Nick's eyes strayed to the guy's face and he almost dropped his drink. For a few moments his head swam and he couldn't seem to force any oxygen into his lungs. Had someone spiked his drink? What was it that caused hallucinations? Ketamine, that was it. Someone must have spiked his whisky with ketamine. Because there was no other explanation for the fact that the guy he'd been eyeing up, the guy he'd all but decided to try and get into bed that evening, was his brother's best friend, Cain. *Fuck!* Bailey had mentioned a Cain. Except, weren't they all meant to adopt different names? He didn't know an awful lot about adult film stars, but he knew that. Everyone knew that. And Cain was hot. Really hot. He shook his head, hoping to clear the fog that had descended over his brain.

As if sensing his stare, Cain lifted his head, the smile he'd been wearing sliding straight off his face. Nick got to watch the whole gamut of emotions cross the other man's face. It started with shock, Cain clearly struggling to process what his eyes were telling him, much as Nick himself had just experienced. Then the color drained from his face and he looked as if he didn't know what to do with himself. He kept dragging his gaze away from Nick's face, only for it to return moments later. Then he didn't even try anymore, the two of them staring at each other across the room.

What was Nick supposed to do now? What was the standard procedure for discovering your brother's best friend made porn? Leave? Talk to him? Continue to just stand there and do nothing? The worst thing was that the dirty fantasies he'd been having before realizing who it was, hadn't gone away. They'd just shifted in perception so that now they seemed ever dirtier.

Cain didn't seem to know what to do either. So they continued staring at each other for a long time. An uncomfortably long time. The spell was only broken when Bailey materialized next to Nick. "Oh, you found one you like. Thank God for that. I thought you were going to be a wallflower all evening." Before he could protest, Nick found himself steered in Cain's direction until there was no longer a space between the two of them, Bailey pushing his way through the crowd in a way that only he could get away with.

"Hello, darling." That was aimed at Cain. "I'd like to introduce you to my friend, Nick. He's a little shy. And, Nick, this absolute hunk of gorgeousness is Cain. Best body at EagerBoyz, I'm sure you'll agree." He leaned in conspiratorially close to Cain, his lips hovering by his ear as he spoke in a pronounced stage whisper. "Don't tell Angel I said that though. I'll be saying the same thing to him when I meet him." He turned and scanned the room, seemingly oblivious to the tension between the two men he'd just introduced. "If I can find him, that is. I've searched every corner and there seems to be absolutely no sign of him so far. I'll keep looking though. I don't give up that easily." He pursed his lips as he finally seemed to realize that there was something not quite right going on in front of him, his gaze darting between Nick and Cain. "Not going to say hello?"

Nick cleared his throat. Given the numerous pairs of eyes on them, he needed to say something. "We've already met." *Major fucking understatement.*

"Oh!" Bailey arched a brow. "I see. I guess I'll leave you two to reacquaint yourselves, then."

Nick nodded, fighting against the urge to demand that Bailey stay exactly where he was and fix the mess he'd created by bringing him to the party in the first place. Instead, he focused on the shiny material that made up the back of Bailey's waistcoat for as long as he could before he was swallowed up by the crowd again, presumably to resume his search for Angel. Whoever the hell he was. When Nick couldn't avoid it any longer, he returned his gaze to Cain, who still looked as if someone had slapped him in the face with a wet fish, his cheeks flushed and his stare glazed. Nick finished the rest of the whisky, never more grateful for the burn of alcohol as it slid down his esophagus. "We should probably talk."

Cain managed a curt nod before seeming to make an effort to gather himself. He scanned the group still clustered in front of him, their eyes wide with curiosity. "Can we have a minute, please?"

There were a few faces that appeared as if they wanted to argue, but the majority melted away, not too far, but at least far enough to clear a small space around the two of them. It wasn't exactly privacy but it would have to do. Nick opened his mouth to speak twice, but both times closed it again without words coming out. In the end, it was Cain who spoke first. "This is awkward."

Nick let out a small laugh. "Yeah, isn't it?" Neither of them were doing a good job of being able to look at each other. Nick had found a spot on the wall, blessedly devoid of pornographic artwork, and Cain's eyes kept darting God knows where. "So, you make porn?"

Cain crossed his arms before just as quickly uncrossing them, Nick doing his best not to let the movement bring his attention to Cain's very bare chest. The same chest that he'd been practically writing poetry about minutes earlier. Cain finally answered. "Erm... yeah."

His gaze kept flicking over to the same place on the wall before just as quickly looking away. Spending a lot of time in the courtroom meant that Nick prided himself on being a bit of a body language expert. So he didn't need a judge or jury to tell him that Cain was trying so hard not to look at something that he couldn't stop looking at it. Nick automatically turned and stared at the picture that contained two men. It was a fucking scene, the bottom's legs over the top's shoulders, his hands gripping onto the other man's biceps as he got his ass plowed. It left absolutely nothing to the imagination. Why Cain seemed so fascinated with it though, Nick had no idea. The view of the bottom's face was blocked by his partner's back, only a shock of dark hair on the pillow visible. There was no question that the picture was hot and it was one of Nick's favorite positions to fuck in, but it really wasn't the time for Cain to be so fascinated with it. They had more important things to discuss. Then in a rush, Nick suddenly got it. "Oh, Jesus! That's you, isn't it?"

He didn't need to wait for Cain to answer, the fact that his cheeks had turned beetroot red said more than any words could. Cain swallowed, the action seeming to take far more effort than it should have done. "Can you stop looking at it, please?"

Nick couldn't. No matter how much he tried to drag his eyes away from it, he just couldn't do it. It should have lost its appeal now that he knew the identity of one of the men in the picture. But it hadn't, and for some reason he'd started to picture himself replacing the top, and his cock pressed against the front of his trousers in a bid to come out and play.

"Nick?"

There was an awful lot of pleading in that one word. Nick forced himself to look elsewhere, but it was like a siren on the rocks trying to drag him back again, begging him to just take one more look. "Why don't we step outside where we can talk without people staring at us, and where there are no..." His eyes flicked back to the picture of Cain getting fucked. "...distractions."

Chapter Five

CAIN

The party had proved far more enjoyable than Cain had expected it to be. He'd rolled his eyes when Evan had decreed that they should all be shirtless, but he had to admit that the attention was nice. Anyone that said they got tired of admiring glances and people who wanted to talk about his workout regime and diet was a liar. Rather than feeling like a prize stallion being eyed up for breeding purposes, he felt like some sort of movie star. Some of the women were even blushing while speaking to him. It was just a shame that he didn't swing that way. Ever. Some of the other guys did. He even suspected that there were a few among the ranks who were far more into women than they were guys, the lure of the salary making them pretend that it was the other way around.

The other bonus was that Blaze seemed to have stayed quiet about his outside interests and hadn't painted him as a total geek. Not yet anyway. Unless the other guys were too busy strutting their stuff tonight to give it much attention. He had a scene booked with Erik next week. He guessed he'd find out then what light Blaze had painted him in. Maybe he'd be lucky and Blaze wouldn't deem it worth the time or energy to gossip about him. He somehow doubted it though. Blaze wasn't exactly known for his circumspection.

So all in all, he'd been having a great time. Up until the point when it had all come crashing down around his ears. He'd had that sixth sense thing where your skin starts prickling and you know someone is watching you. He'd tried to ignore it, figuring it was just someone eyeing him up. But it had reached the point where he couldn't anymore, where the temptation to find out who it was, and what they wanted, had become too much, and he'd searched out the source of the interest. As soon as he found it, he'd wished he hadn't—his blood running cold and any noise in the room fading to a dull roar. If he'd ever been asked to compile a list of people who would never attend a party like this, then the name Nicholas Hackett would surely have appeared right at the top. Except there he was, staring right at Cain, his fingers gripping the glass he held so tightly that his knuckles were white. Cain's first instinct had been to run and hide, and he'd had to remind himself that he wasn't twelve years old, that he was a fully grown adult who had to face up to his issues no matter how unpalatable they might be. It was doubtful he could have gotten his legs to work anyway in order to flee when they'd become rooted to the spot. It was all he could do to keep breathing for those first few seconds. Anything beyond that had been firmly diverted into the "not possible" category.

The conversation that had followed had been awkward as fuck, Cain hoping that at any moment he'd wake up and discover that his best friend's brother and the man he'd had a crush on for the last ten years hadn't just stumbled his way into discovering his secret. And then, of course, there was that damn picture of himself. That he'd happened to be standing right next to. He'd been so paranoid about Nick noticing it and making the connection, that in the end he'd brought the other man's attention to it like the stupid idiot he apparently was. And then what had seemed just awkward before had been nothing in comparison to Nick staring at the picture for so damn long that Cain had given serious consideration to the best place at the party to curl up and die. Because you could die from embarrassment, right? It had certainly felt like it.

"Why don't we step outside where we can talk without people staring at us, and where there are no... distractions."

Cain had agreed to Nick's suggestion. It might not solve the excruciating awkwardness between the two of them, but it would get him away from that picture, and put an end to the interested stares that kept flicking between them as onlookers tried to work out what the deal was between them.

Nick led the way to the door, Cain grabbing a glass of champagne from one of the passing waiters and downing it in just a few swallows. It was a bad idea especially when he'd already drunk half a glass, but God knows he needed it.

It was quieter in the corridor with only a few people milling around, most of them just passing through.

Nick exhaled noisily as he leaned back against the wall, his hands tucked under his armpits in a defensive stance, his gaze fixed sightlessly on the wall opposite. Cain stared at him, bracing himself for whatever was about to come out of Nick's mouth and wishing there was some way they could just skip the conversation entirely. As the seconds stretched between them, he realized there was something worse than a conversation though—silence. Cain shifted uncomfortably, the movement causing Nick's gaze to sweep back to him as if he'd almost forgotten he was there. His brow furrowed. "Does Theo know?"

"That I make porn?" It was a stupid question. What else was he going to be talking about?

He gave a curt nod.

Cain shook his head. "Not yet. I was going to tell him. I've wanted to for some time, but... I don't know... there just hasn't seemed to be a good time. You know what Theo can be like. He can turn even the smallest thing into a big drama. I wasn't sure how he'd take it. I *will* tell him though." Except that hung in the balance now, didn't it? He'd only get to tell Theo himself if he managed to get there first, before Nick had a chance.

"What about the restaurant?"

Cain frowned, the question making very little sense. "What about it?"

"I thought that's what you wanted to do with your life. Learn the workings of a restaurant so you can maybe own one of your own one day."

It was difficult for Cain to hold back a laugh. The lawyer in Nick always saw everything in black and white. Nick had always struggled with gray areas. He'd forgotten that about him, given how little time they'd spent together over the last few years. "Buying a restaurant takes money. Where do you think that money's going to come from? I could get a loan, but then I'd be stuck paying it off for the rest of my life. Why do that if I don't have to? Porn pays well. Very well." He spat out the last sentence much more defensively than he'd planned to. He might be embarrassed at the way his secret had come out but there was no way that he was going to let Nick make him feel ashamed. He held his head up high and forced himself to look him straight in the eye. "Besides, it's fun."

"Is it?"

Nick looked so confused by the concept that Cain almost felt sorry for him. He brushed the feeling away, his head starting to buzz from the rapid injection of champagne. What had he been thinking? If there were three things that really didn't mix, it was him, Nick, and drunkenness. He'd spent years avoiding being drunk around Nick just in case anything slipped out that shouldn't. "Of course it's fun. It's sex with gorgeous men. What's not to like about that?"

Nick looked less than convinced. "Yeah, but... you know... on camera. It's just a bit..."

Cain couldn't stop his eyes from narrowing on Nick's face. "A bit what?"

"I don't know." Nick's eyes skated over him before he quickly averted his gaze, going back to his scrutiny of the wall. "Can't you put a shirt on or something?"

The words stung, Cain's hands curling into fists that wanted nothing more than to find out what Nick's face might feel like if they made contact. *Of all the jumped-up uptight things to say.* "Oh, I'm sorry if my bare chest offends you. I'd assume given that you came to a *porn* party that you were expecting some bare skin. So I guess it's just mine that upsets you so much."

"I didn't want to come."

The words were muttered under Nick's breath, so it took Cain a few moments to decipher them. "So why did you?"

"Bailey made me."

The words were delivered in such a petulant fashion that again Cain was tempted to laugh. It couldn't be healthy to be oscillating so rapidly between anger and amusement. One minute he wanted to punch Nick and the next he wanted to... well, he wasn't even going to think about that. At least the mention of Bailey was sobering. He'd known he was there. How could he not, given that it was Bailey, in his ignorance, who'd tried to introduce the two of them. If he was honest though, he'd harbored a secret hope that that was just a coincidence. "Oh yes, Bailey." The words dripped with all the burning jealousy he felt when it came to the blond man who'd practically been Nick's shadow for the last few years from the photographs he'd seen. Whether it was the champagne, the shock of discovery, Nick's prudish attitude, or a combination of all of them, Cain couldn't have said. All he knew was that ten years of repressed feelings were suddenly bubbling up inside him and he couldn't bring himself to give a fuck what Nick thought. It was never going to happen between them, so therefore he had nothing to lose.

Nick rubbed his chin, his brows pinched together. "Why did you say it like that? He's a good friend. He's the one who wanted to come tonight. It certainly wasn't my idea."

"Friend!" The word came out so sharply Cain may as well have delivered it with a whip. "You're always photographed with him. I don't know why the two of you deny being together."

"Because we're not together."

Cain wasn't having it. He needed an outlet for all the things he'd been bottling up and Bailey seemed like a suitable target if ever there was one. The man was gorgeous, rich and had never had to work a day in his life, and Nick seemed to be at his beck and call. Yeah, it was official; Cain hated him with a passion. "Right. Course you're not."

"We're not." Nick's jaw clenched as he jerked a hand back in the direction of the party. "He came here for one thing and one thing only tonight, to try and get into as many porn stars' pants as he can. I'm sure if you ask nicely you can have a turn too. I don't know what kind of relationships you think I have, but I'm not into sharing." His face hardened. "Anyway, how did we get onto this subject. We were meant to be talking about you. I have no idea what my love life has got to do with you? Why the hell would *you* be interested in it?"

The words were like someone twisting a knife in Cain's gut. "You really don't know?"

Nick gave an exaggerated shrug which just riled Cain up even more. He should walk away. He should go back to the party and talk to people who were interested in him. He should pick one of them up and take them home. It wasn't like he'd been short on offers already. There were a handful of men who'd made it blatantly clear that they were up for a bit of fun with Cain. He tried to picture their faces but all he could see was Nick. This man had a lot to answer for. How dare he stand there cool as a cucumber, looking at Cain as if he didn't have a clue what could possibly be wrong with him?

He advanced on Nick, making the other man take a step back. A red haze filled Cain's mind, obliterating any last iota of common sense. "You're really going to stand there and pretend that you didn't notice when I followed you around like a lost sheep? That you were clueless when I always made a beeline to talk to you at family events. Oh, come on, Nick. You're a lawyer for God's sake! You can't be that blind. Nobody's that blind." His voice was starting to slur. Cain could hear it, but he was powerless to stop it. If he'd stayed sober, he had a feeling that this conversation would have gone a very different way. He'd started now though, so there was no going back. There was only seeing it through to the bitter end. And he might as well go down in flames. "I had a thing for you. I *have* a thing for you. A thing that won't go away no matter how much I will it to, or no matter how many times you treat me like another kid brother or call me squirt." The thought suddenly struck him that at no point during this conversation had Nick called him that. How strange! That had to be a first. "So yeah, there you have it."

Nick swallowed, the action bringing Cain's attention to his throat. A throat that he'd have given anything to get the opportunity to lick and kiss. When Nick spoke, it was slowly and deliberately as if he was trying to be very careful with his words. "I knew you had a crush on me when you were younger, but I figured it wore off."

"Yeah, well, it didn't." Cain surged forward, pressing Nick against the wall. Everything inside him screamed "yes" at the sensation of Nick's body against his. It didn't even matter that Nick wore a shirt. The cool fabric felt fantastic against his bare, overheated skin. He was running a fever and there was only one cure, and it was right in front of him, staring at him with wide eyes. Cain was feeling reckless and to hell with the consequences. He leaned closer, remembering all the times he'd dreamt about what Nick's lips might feel like against his own, both awake and asleep. It was time to find out. In fact, it was way past time. He was tantalizingly close to realizing that dream when Nick's hand squeezed between their bodies, his fingers spreading over Cain's chest and holding him at bay. "Cain, don't."

Cain couldn't stop the sound of frustration from escaping from his mouth. He'd been so damn close. He glared at Nick, a part of him recognizing how unfair that was. It wasn't as if

Nick had asked him to kiss him, or led him on in any way. Cain worked to fight past the fog in his brain, the fog that demanded that he ignore what Cain had said and kiss him. Just this once. Just so he'd know and he could keep that as a memory. He wasn't a damn caveman though. He forced himself to take a step back, the world feeling cold without Nick's body heat merging with his. "I suppose you want me to apologize."

Nick shook his head, the expression on his face pained. "No. It's just..." He ran a hand through his hair. "You wouldn't want me, not really, not if you knew me properly."

Cain had thought that nothing could hurt more than rejection. He'd been wrong. Being told you didn't even know a person who'd been in your life for over a decade hurt far more. He retreated back to his own side of the corridor, using the time to try and decipher the cryptic statement. Maybe Nick hadn't meant what it sounded like? But no matter what positive spin Cain tried to put on them, the words still came out the same. "What do you mean? I do know you. I've known you for years. We go way back."

"You should go back to the party."

It felt like there was an actual physical pain in Cain's chest. Was this what heartbreak felt like? There was a reason Cain had guarded his bad case of unrequited love so zealously and for such a long time. And going by what Nick had said about him knowing he'd had a crush on him as a teenager, but thinking he'd grown out of it, he'd done an excellent job of it. Nick's face swam in front of his eyes for a moment. There was no way he was going to give him the satisfaction of knowing that he was upset. He drew himself up to his full height and looked Nick in the eye. "Good idea. Maybe I will check out your friend, Bailey.

If he's as friendly as you say he is, then he sounds like he could give me a really good time."

If he'd been hoping that Nick might raise some objection to the insinuation that he was going to sleep with his friend, he was left disappointed at Nick's silence. It was time to make a retreat and lick his wounds. Forcing his feet to move, he turned around and started to walk down the corridor, raising a hand in a casual wave without looking back. "See you around, Nick."

"Cain?"

Hope flowered in his heart. He halted and spun around. "Yeah?"

"Please don't drink any more tonight. Alcohol's never had a great effect on you. I still remember covering for you and Theo when you both got drunk at fifteen, and you'd only had one beer."

Cain gave him the finger and carried on walking. Nicholas Hackett could go to hell. He didn't care if he never saw him again.

Chapter Six

NICK

Nick rolled onto his back, groaning at the dull throb in his head at the shift in position. After the altercation with Cain, he'd left the party, but instead of going straight home, he'd decided that it would be a good idea to head to a bar and get ridiculously drunk instead.

His hand reached out blindly, hoping to stop the insistent noise that was responsible for rousing him from his stupor. After a few passes that resulted in zero success, his fingers curled around the familiar surface of his phone. Dragging it toward him, he was forced to crack open one eye in order to hit the answer button. He brought it to his ear, wondering if he'd eaten sand last night. It certainly felt like it. "What?" Any croakier and he would have been a fully paid-up member of the frog family.

"Good thing I'm not one of your clients if you're going to answer the phone with so little decorum."

Bailey. He rolled back onto his side, leaving the phone squashed beneath his cheek. If he was lucky, he might accidentally press something that would terminate the call and he could go back to sleep. "This is not my work phone. Therefore, there's zero chance of clients calling me on it. Just annoying people who wake me up."

"You do know what time it is?"

Nick didn't have a bloody clue. He seemed to remember climbing in a cab at about two in the morning, and then things after that were even hazier, so he had no idea what time he'd actually gotten to bed. "This is a shit quiz. Do I even get multiple choice options?"

"I'll go one better than that. I'll just tell you. Midday. This is the third time I've tried to call you."

"So maybe you should have taken a hint."

A sigh echoed over the line. "I'm going to assume that all the attitude aimed my way is something to do with you being a tad hungover. Which is strange really, considering you did a runner at the party."

Nick made an attempt to open his eyes, but as he hadn't bothered to close his curtains and since it was apparently midday, the light was far too bright. If there was one thing he'd learned in the courtroom, it was that the best form of offense was often attack. "I'm surprised you noticed. Did your hunt for a porn star to warm your bed not go too well?"

"It went absolutely fine. A hundred percent successful, thank you very much."

Nausea that had absolutely nothing to do with the alcohol in his system settled in Nick's stomach as he recalled Cain's parting words about seeking out Bailey. Had he meant it? Was that why Bailey was calling? To boast about his night with Cain? "Who with?" He tried to tell himself that it didn't matter if Bailey said Cain's name. That it was none of his business. But he couldn't quite seem to get the concept to sit right in his brain. That was the problem with hangovers. They stopped you from thinking rationally.

"A gentleman never tells."

"Good thing you're not a gentleman, then." Nick summoned all his strength and lifted his head from the pillow, counting to ten in an attempt to avoid asking the question hovering on his lips. On eight, he conceded defeat. "Was it Cain?" Silence followed his question. "Bailey?"

"No, it wasn't, but I was just thinking about how fascinating I find your question, darling."

Nick let his head thud back onto the pillow, telling himself that the flood of relief was a natural reaction to the news that a family friend hadn't become tangled in Bailey's web. "Fascinating, right."

Bailey chuckled. "Here's what's going to happen. I'm going to give you an hour to turn yourself back into a human being, and then I'm going to call you again. Then we're going to have a little chat about all the weird energy that was flying back and forth between the two of you, and why after you'd dragged him outside, you immediately left and he came back to the party with a face like thunder. Oh, and, Nick, just so you know, if you don't answer your phone, I'll come around and see you instead. Your choice. One hour, Nick."

Nick grunted, and was still trying to think of a suitable comeback when the line went dead. *Fucking Bailey!* He brought the phone to his face, squinting at the time just in case Bailey had exaggerated but it was indeed past midday. He needed breakfast and coffee, but unfortunately both of those things required getting out of bed. Taking a deep breath, he heaved himself up enough that he could twist around and put his feet on the floor, the duvet falling away. Then he sat and waited for the monkey in his head to stop banging the cymbals together. Breakfast, coffee, *and* painkillers.

He glanced down. *Fuck!* In the cold light of day with a thumping hangover, white lace panties weren't what he needed to see. Drunk him had obviously felt like indulging himself even more once he'd gotten home. He had a sneaking suspicion who he'd been thinking about as well. Managing to stand, he quickly stripped them off, shoving them at the bottom of the laundry basket before going to take a shower.

An hour later, he felt a lot better. So much so that when Bailey called back, he was able to answer the phone far more cheerfully than he had done earlier.

"There he is! The grunting Neanderthal that I spoke to earlier has left the building and my friend has returned."

There was only one good answer to that level of sarcasm. "Fuck off."

Bailey laughed. "You're right, no more sparkling repartee. Let's get straight to the point. I have after all got other things I need to do today. Why didn't you tell me you knew any porn stars?"

Nick leaned on the kitchen counter, resting his chin on his fist. "Because I wasn't aware I did, that's why." Bailey made an encouraging noise, a clear instruction that he should carry on. "Cain is a friend of my brother's. He's almost like a..." He hesitated, trying to gauge the honesty of his response before saying it. "...brother to me as well." They weren't brotherly feelings he'd been having toward him before he'd worked out who it was though, were they? Not unless he had another unpalatable sexual predilection on top of the underwear. "I had no idea he'd been making porn. He'd kept it a secret."

Bailey let out a long, low whistle. "Well, that definitely explains the awkwardness between the two of you. You could have cut the atmosphere with a knife. I hope you didn't go all judgmental on him."

"No!" Had he? Maybe a bit. But porn stars were all well and good until you were confronted by a ten-foot picture of someone you know getting fucked.

"So… you were so shocked you had to leave?"

"There was other stuff as well."

"Spill."

"He… Cain told me he'd had a thing for me for years. I mean I knew he did as a kid. He was pretty obvious about it, but I've barely seen him recently. And then he tried to kiss me."

"Oh, you lucky dog. Cain is fucking gorgeous. Have you seen that body? Well, I guess you must have with the two of you going way back. I'm actually jealous, and I don't think I've ever said that to you before. Hey, do you remember me saying to you that he always looks a bit sad when he's on camera? Maybe that's it. He's been thinking about the one guy he couldn't have. You. Except now he can and the two of you can—"

"I turned him down."

"Why?"

Nick shook his head. "You must have missed the bit where I told you he was a friend of my brother's. He and Theo are like that"—he held up two crossed fingers even though he knew Bailey couldn't see him—"besides, you know why. Even if I was interested, which I'm not, I bet his crush would soon wear off once he knew the truth about me. And then he'd tell my brother, and I do not need my little brother looking at me like that."

"Like what?" Bailey's voice was unusually soft.

"Like I'm a massive pervert."

"Nick, we've had this same conversation a hundred times. You're not a pervert. You happen to have a fetish. Lots of people have fetishes. With some people it's feet, whereas for others it's... I don't know bondage or electrostimulation or something. You just happen to get off on wearing women's underwear. It's not the huge crime you make it out to be. Look at me! I wear women's stuff. Like the heels I wore last night."

Nick swallowed around the lump in his throat. "Not underwear though."

Bailey sighed. "No, but I would if I wanted to."

"And the things you wear don't turn you on. They're just for decoration. It's not the same."

A note of frustration crept into Bailey's voice. "Maybe not. I wasn't saying it was."

Nick wasn't done with his arguments. "You can get away with it. You're a socialite. I'm a lawyer. Who's going to take me seriously in court if they're picturing me wearing silk or lace?"

"I'm not suggesting that you alert the media, or flash your sexy undies in court. I just wish you'd believe that there are people in this world who can keep a secret and that aren't going to be scandalized just because you like the feel of a bit of satin against your cock. I know some of your past boyfriends were dicks. But not everyone is like that. You're going to have to let someone in eventually and give them a chance."

Deep down, Nick knew that Bailey was right, but he made it sound so simple when it was anything but. The problem with trusting people was that you didn't find out whether you could trust them or not until afterwards. He wouldn't have told the boyfriends at all, if he hadn't thought he could trust them. Although, to give them their due, neither had shouted his penchant for dressing in panties to the rooftops. So maybe they could be trusted. They just hadn't understood it enough to want to stick around. And they hadn't been able to get their heads around the fact that nothing about Nick had actually changed: he was still the same guy underneath.

As much as he appreciated Bailey trying to help, he didn't want to talk about it anymore. They'd just go around in circles with Bailey getting more and more annoyed at him. Bailey wouldn't be happy until Nick could repeat "I'm not a pervert" a hundred times over and actually believe it. Therefore, a subject change was in order. "What are you up to tonight? Having a quiet night in?"

Bailey gave a throaty chuckle. "Of course not. I have a porn star coming round. One taste was not enough for them."

"Oh, wow! Look at you seeing someone two nights in a row. Careful! You might start catching feelings."

"Not likely." Bailey's tone was dry and filled with cynicism. "Who needs sex complicated by the f word. He can come and share his body with me until I get tired of him and then he can get lost."

"Ouch!" Whoever he was, Nick felt sorry for him. The poor guy wasn't going to know what hit him.

He thought about pressing Bailey for a name again but it was likely the name wouldn't mean anything anyway. Curiosity would only lead him to looking the guy up on the EagerBoyz site, and he had no intention of going anywhere near it. He'd seen enough of Cain naked to last him a lifetime. He ignored the voice inside his head calling him a liar. It could go to hell.

The conversation came to a natural end a few minutes later, Bailey insisting on letting him know that he needed to go and pluck some stray hairs down below before his date that wasn't a date.

After the conversation with Bailey had ended, Cain was still on his mind. Nick thumbed through the numbers on his phone until he found the right one. Not giving himself time for second-guessing, he pressed call. It rang and rang, voicemail finally kicking in. Nick didn't bother leaving a message. He tried twice more over the next hour but with the same result.

Perhaps a text would be better? Less pressure.

Nick: *Hi, Cain, I just wanted to apologize if I said or did anything that upset you last night. I didn't mean to. Call me and we can have a chat and clear things up. Nick.*

He agonized about whether to add a kiss or not at the end, deciding that after the night's revelations, it wouldn't be a good idea.

Just like the phone calls had, the message went unanswered.

Chapter Seven

CAIN

The scene from the hotel window was picture postcard perfect, all rolling hills and lush countryside as far as the eye could see. It was a far cry from the gray streets of London, and they were only in Hertfordshire. It should have been relaxing, but Cain felt anything but. A sharp rap on the door proved just how jumpy he was when he almost took flight.

Heart still pounding, he crossed the room to open it, Theo pushing his way in before the door was even fully open. Cain let the door close, turning around to find Theo standing with his hands on his hips, glaring at him. Pretending not to notice, Cain picked up the tiny kettle that came with the room and held it out in invitation. "Cup of tea? I'll probably have to boil it twice if I have one as well. They're obviously more used to people that drink out of thimbles."

The glare became even more pronounced. "What's going on, Cain?"

He played dumb. "What do you mean?"

"You've been AWOL for the last couple of weeks. Not picking up your phone. Not answering my texts. And then Carol told me that you'd called her and tried to wriggle your way out of coming here for the wedding."

"I'm here, aren't I?"

"Yeah, hiding in your room instead of drinking with us at the bar. And Carol said she had to fake cry in order to get you here."

Cain frowned as he thought back to the call. She'd seemed inconsolable on the phone, feeding him what had apparently been a load of bullshit about how last-minute nerves had kicked in. She'd even said she wasn't sure whether she should still marry Rory, and then gone on to talk for at least ten minutes about how she needed her friends there to support her—all of them. Especially Cain, because he was very important to her. She'd made out that he gave fantastic advice because he was far more understanding and sensitive than anyone else she knew.

Actually, now that he thought about it, Cain should have smelled a rat. It had Theo's touch stamped all over it. He'd probably been in the background feeding her the lines and egging her on. Theo's middle name should have been manipulation. He filled the kettle at the small sink in the bathroom, using it as an excuse to avoid looking Theo's way while he asked the question that he needed to. "Have you seen your brother?" He risked a glance Theo's way once the words were out of his mouth and he couldn't take them back.

Theo's eyebrows knitted together. "When? Today?"

Cain shrugged, pretending a great fascination in one of the small milk cartons that the hotel provided. They were difficult to open, but not that difficult. "I just meant recently?"

"Yeah, course I've seen him recently. He's my brother. We had dinner last week. Why?"

Cain added milk to the cups and poured the water in. "What did you talk about?"

"I dunno... his work. I switched off for most of that, though, because... boring. I don't need to know what criminals Super Nick has put behind bars this week. Mum and Dad obviously, because we kind of have those in common. Erm... not much else, really. Oh, and he's thinking of buying a new car. He showed me some pictures but you know cars are not really my thing. I don't think he appreciated my feedback on colors and seat fabric. I told him about the latest World of Warcraft expansion pack. I think that was when he nearly nodded off."

It should have been a relief that Nick hadn't said anything. Cain had managed to convince himself that that's why Theo had been so easy to avoid, that Nick had told Theo everything and that Theo was mad at Cain as a result. But it seemed that his friend had just been busy, which left Cain right back at square one, thinking that maybe it might have been easier in some way if the information had already been out there. In fact, it couldn't be worse really. Now, his best friend's brother knew something that Theo didn't—and had for weeks. If it did ever come out, and Cain wasn't naive, it had to eventually, that would just make it even worse. He held out the cup of tea to Theo.

Despite Theo eyeing it like Cain had just passed across a live hand grenade, he took it. "I don't want tea. I've just been drinking beer. And I intend to get back to it once I've got to the bottom of why you're being so squirrely. So why would I want to stop for a cup of tea?"

Ignoring his friend's grumbling, Cain considered his options. It would make a lot more sense to wait until after the wedding was over before telling Theo. Then they wouldn't be stuck together for the whole weekend should Theo not take it that well. But Nick was also going to be there this weekend—hence his reasons for not wanting to come—and there'd be alcohol flowing so just because he hadn't said anything yet didn't mean he wouldn't. Cain's head was swimming. *Tell him. Don't tell him.* The two options kept cycling through his brain with neither of them seeming like the better option.

"I make porn."

Okay, blurting it out like that had never been in the cards. A gentle lead-in before gradually working up to it would have been a far better choice. But the words were out there now and there was no taking them back.

Theo's eyes went so wide that for a moment his face was completely dominated by them. "Porn!" The cup in his hands wobbled and Cain quickly snatched it back before the contents ended up all over the hotel's cream-colored carpet. Theo continued to stare at him. "Porn like what? Like sex-on-camera porn? With people? Where? Why? Who?" He waved his hands about like he didn't know what to do with them. "Give me the tea."

Cain dutifully passed the cup back, watching with amusement as his friend downed it like it was a shot of whisky. He'd imagined this scenario a thousand times, and he'd imagined every possible reaction, from Theo getting angry to him being upset. He'd never foreseen him losing the ability to make sense though. "What other kind of porn is there other than having sex on camera with people?"

His friend backed away, slowly lowering himself to sit gingerly on the bed. "Animals." He held up a hand, a stricken look on his face. "Wait. Delete that word from your memory bank. I did not just suggest that you have sex with animals for money. That would be a terrible thing to say."

"Consider it deleted."

Theo exhaled noisily. "So, porn... that's, yeah. That's a thing that you do, is it?"

Cain leaned back against the chest of drawers, needing the support. Once Theo got over the initial shock, then his true feelings were probably going to come out. "Yeah, that's what I do." He braced himself. "I've done it for the past year."

"A year!" Theo still seemed as if he was trying to wrap his head around Cain's first announcement. A few seconds went by before his expression changed to one of hurt. "You haven't told me for a year. Why not?"

That was a question Cain had asked himself on numerous occasions. At first, he'd just wanted to wait. After all, it could have ended up being something he only did a couple of times, and then there would have been nothing to tell. And after that, well, he'd had the problem that it had already been a secret for some time. He answered as honestly as he could. "Because... I wasn't sure what you'd make of it. Whether you'd approve, and you're my best friend, so your approval means the world to me. You know that."

Theo nodded slowly, staring into space for the best part of a minute as if he was slowly working some stuff out. Finally, he spoke. "I have questions."

Cain crossed his arms over his chest. "Go on." It wouldn't be Theo without a barrage of questions. He just hoped it was information he was prepared to share with his straight best friend.

"Does it pay a lot? Are you like really rich now? Is it one guy or lots? Are you going to carry on doing it?"

Cain thought about it. "A fair amount. Not enough for me to be rich but enough for cash flow to be a lot easier. One guy so far, but there's a couple of group scenes coming up that I might be chosen for. And yes, I'm going to keep doing it."

"Huh!" Theo's brow suddenly furrowed. "Why were you asking if I'd seen Nick? What's any of this got to do with my brother?" His jaw dropped. "Oh my God! Has Nick been making porn?"

Cain couldn't help it, he laughed. "Your brother's a lawyer. Of course he's not making porn. I really don't think those two things would mix." An image came to mind of Nick laid out on the huge bed they used to film, his suit rumpled and a come-hither smile on his face. Cain shook his head to clear it. Any sexual thoughts about Nick were strictly banned. There was a reason he'd ignored his calls and texts: he didn't even want to speak to him, never mind see him. As far as he was concerned, Nick needed to stay the hell away from him at the wedding, and that would do them both a favor.

Theo held his hand out, waggling his fingers in a command. "Give me the other cup of tea." Cain watched in bemusement as it went the same way as the first. He waited until Theo had placed the cup on the nightstand, his words cautious. "So, are you cool with it? Me making porn, that is?"

Theo gave him a narrow-eyed stare. "I'll tell you what I'm not cool with, you keeping secrets from me. We're definitely going to be discussing that when we're not at a wedding. As for the porn..." His face screwed up. "I guess so. It's your body. You can do whatever you want with it. Just don't show any of it to me, okay. I've seen your bare ass in real life. I don't need to see it on the screen."

Cain let out a breath he hadn't even realized he'd been holding, relief loosening his chest. "Agreed. I can't say that I particularly want you to see it either." It probably wouldn't be as bad as Nick's face had been when he'd seen that print of Cain getting fucked though. He could still see his expression clearly—a strange mix of absolute horror and some other emotion that Cain hadn't quite been able to identify. "And just to be completely upfront with you, the reason it's linked to your brother is because he found out, and I thought he would have told you."

Theo shook his head. "No, he didn't say anything. How the hell did Nick find out?"

"He was at a party that the studio held. His little socialite friend apparently dragged him along. At least that's what he told me." Cain couldn't keep the edge out of his voice when he mentioned Bailey. Nick might claim there was nothing going on between the two of them, but he still wasn't sure he believed it. The two of them were far too close.

"Bailey?"

Cain nodded.

Theo smiled. "Sounds like Bailey's idea of a good time. So that's why you were trying to avoid the wedding, in case Nick had told everyone?"

Cain grimaced. "Partly." When Theo's brow lifted in a silent question, he elaborated. "I'd had a drink and you know what I'm like when I've had a drink. I kind of told him that I had a thing for him, and then I tried to..." He paused, the memory still too raw and the fingers of humiliation working their way through his body, even though it had been a couple of weeks.

"Tried to what?"

"Kiss him."

Theo's eyes went wide again. "And what happened?"

"What do you think happened? He pushed me away. Muttered some crap about me not really knowing him. It was excruciatingly embarrassing. It still is. That's why I don't want to be here. Because Nick is here and I don't need him looking at me in that disapproving way he's perfected over the years just because we can't all be as perfect as he is."

"You haven't spoken to him since?"

Cain shook his head. "He's tried to call and text a few times but I didn't answer because I had no idea what I was supposed to say. I'm meant to be sitting at the same table as him tomorrow. You've got to get Carol to move me. I know it's last minute, but there must be someone she can swap me with. I can't sit near Nick. Not after I made such a huge fool of myself."

"But then you won't be sitting with me." Theo looked so crestfallen at the notion that it was all Cain could do not to smile. Yeah, Theo didn't give a damn about him making porn. Their friendship was still intact. No doubt he'd bring it up again when he wanted something, reminding him that he'd kept the secret from him for a whole year. But they were good and that was the main thing. At least that solved one problem. Now he just needed to deal with the other one. It was going to be bad enough having to be in the same room as Nick without being mere meters away, and if that meant having to surgically separate himself from his best friend, then that was the price he'd have to pay. "Please, Theo. For me."

Theo's sigh was long and dramatic. "Fine." You owe me some serious gaming time though. You know that, right? That's if you're not too busy with all these sexual exploits you've apparently got going on. I've always said you were too hot to be a proper geek."

Cain laughed. Only a fellow geek could say he wasn't geekish enough.

Chapter Eight

NICK

The ceremony had gone off without a hitch, Carol looking resplendent in her simply ivory-white sheath dress. Given that the ceremony had been outdoors in the manor house's grounds, one of the major worries had been that the weather wouldn't hold up. But although it couldn't exactly be classed as fantastic, there'd been no hint of rain and the sun had even broken through the clouds on a couple of occasions.

Nick had been hoping to grab a quick word with Cain before the wedding but Cain's conspicuous absence at the bar where everyone else had congregated the night before had rendered that an impossibility. Due to Cain refusing to respond to messages, or answer his calls, things still felt very unresolved between the two of them. He just wanted a chance to speak to him in person and sort things out, try and make sure it wasn't awkward between the two of them, for Theo's sake if nothing else. Cain might have said that stuff, but it had probably only been the drink talking. It was hard to believe that Cain could really have carried a torch for him for that long without saying something. Hard to believe and hard to get his head around without some very strange feelings he didn't want to think about making themselves known. The sooner he spoke to Cain and they got things back on a friendly footing, the better.

As family members, Nick and Theo had been seated close to the front during the ceremony. He'd expected Cain to be there too. Wherever Theo was, Cain was usually sure to follow and vice versa, but once the ceremony had started and there'd been no sign, Nick had turned to carry out a search through the audience, finally locating Cain seated near the back. Perhaps he'd arrived late and Theo had been too much of a doofus to remember to save a seat for him. Any attempts to catch Cain's eye had failed miserably, Cain continuing to stare straight ahead. He'd looked good though, the charcoal gray suit he wore fitting his broad shoulders perfectly. And Nick couldn't quite force his brain to forget just how broad those shoulders had been when you took clothes out of the equation.

Curiosity had almost gotten the best of him over the last couple of weeks, Nick even going so far as to type half of the porn studio's address into the search bar on his browser before thinking better of it. He hadn't wanted to watch the scenes. But he could just look at some of the pictures, right? Only that had seemed too invasive as well. Like he was somehow spying on Cain without his permission, which was a ridiculous thought. It was public for God's sake. If Cain didn't want people to look at him, then he should never have done it. But then Nick wasn't just people, was he? The arguments had gone round and round in Nick's head, and in the end, despite being extremely tempted, he hadn't looked.

Knowing he'd get to talk to Cain at the reception, he'd given up trying to catch his eye. It wasn't like he could have gotten away with facing in the wrong direction for too long during the ceremony. Carol would have strung him up by his balls should she have noticed. As it was, she'd been too busy staring longingly into Rory's eyes.

Only now that they'd all filed into the specially decorated room for the reception and found their table courtesy of the decorative place name placards, there was someone else seated next to his brother where Cain was supposed to be. Someone Nick didn't even recognize. His gaze searched the room, finally locating Cain right at the other end of the room with his back to him. It was like the ceremony all over again.

Nick leaned across the table, jostling his brother's elbow when he failed to look his way. "Why is Cain over there? He's meant to be sitting here."

Theo gave him a long, hard look. "Oh, so you're going to play innocent, are you? Pretend that you have absolutely no part to play in Cain avoiding you. Why do you think he didn't come to the bar last night? Why do you think he sat somewhere else during the ceremony and isn't here now? Which I shouldn't need to tell you that I'm upset about. So just for the record, he's pissed at you and I'm pissed at you too."

Nick blinked his way through the torrent of words, Theo's set expression telling him that he meant every word. "What did I do?"

Theo's eyebrows rose. "Seriously? He bared his soul to you and you cruelly rejected him."

Nick's lips quirked. He should be used to his brother being dramatic, but he could still surprise him at times. It was probably one of the reasons Bailey's flair for drama was like water off a duck's back to him. He'd had it for years from his own sibling. "I don't remember there being any soul baring."

Theo leaned farther forward and lowered his voice. "He told you he liked you. That he's liked you for years and you rejected him. He didn't go into details, but I got the impression that you were none too gentle about it either. How did you expect him to feel? He feels like an idiot. *You* made him feel like an idiot."

It wasn't difficult to see whose side Theo was on. Anyone else but Cain, and Nick might have felt seriously peeved about it. "It was a difficult night. There were other things going on that had clouded my judgement. He—"

"I know what happened."

Nick searched his brother's face, trying to ascertain exactly what he did know. The antagonism Theo was displaying for Nick daring to turn Cain down masked everything else though. He needed to be careful here. It had been hard enough to keep his mouth shut when the two of them had had dinner. Nick knew what it was like to keep secrets better than anyone though, and there was no way he had any intention of being the one to spill Cain's. "You know about the...?"

Theo checked left and right to make sure that no one else was listening in on their conversation before mouthing the word "porn" across the table.

Well, at least that was something. Nick could stop being paranoid that he'd let something slip to his brother. "And you're fine with it?"

Theo's glare turned even more pronounced. "Yeah, better than you were apparently. Cain didn't say much but I could tell from his face that you weren't great about it. Besides"—Theo pulled a face—"even if I wasn't, you know what Cain's like. He hates being told what to do. If I even thought of suggesting he stop, it would probably have the opposite effect and he'd just do it until he was old and wrinkly."

Guilt gnawed at Nick's stomach. He definitely could have handled it better. "It was a bit of a shock. He was the last person I expected to see there." He swallowed with difficulty. "And there were pictures. Big pictures. Of... you know what?"

Grabbing his glass, Theo downed half of the Prosecco in it. "Okay, too much information. I don't care about the details. All I care about is you sorting things out with Cain. You're making me suffer because you've been a twat. You should already have sorted it out."

"I've been trying." Realizing that in his need to produce a spirited defense, his voice had gotten louder, Nick lowered it again to a whisper. "I've been trying to get into contact with him, but he hasn't been answering. Then I was going to corner him and talk to him last night, but he wasn't there. And now"—he lifted his arm to point across the room—"he's all the way over there. He's not making it easy." Despite Nick stating the truth, Theo's glare hadn't lessened in the slightest. Nick sighed. "But I will talk to him and I'll apologize for perhaps coming across as a little too judgmental."

Theo's eye's narrowed. "And for rejecting him?"

"You make it sound like you want us to get together?" Something clenched in Nick's chest as he voiced the ridiculous notion aloud.

The grimace on Theo's face wasn't difficult to interpret. "God, no! That would be like the weirdest thing ever." The scowl morphed into a grin. "Anyway, Cain's mine. Keep your grubby hands off him. But you know there's ways of turning people down without being a dick about it. Like, oh my God,

I'm so flattered but I've just never looked at you that way. Not spouting some bullshit about him not really knowing you. What were you thinking, coming out with crap like that?"

Somehow, Nick managed to school his face. "He told you that?"

"He tells me everything... eventually. Course he told me that." Theo held his hand up, his fingers crossed. "Cain and I are like that. At least until he started avoiding me because of your dumb ass."

Whatever Nick might have said in response was stalled by the servers arriving at their table with the first course. The next couple of hours were filled with food, wine, speeches, and more wine. Even though Nick had tried to limit himself as much as he could, he had a pretty decent buzz going by the time the formal part of the evening had drawn to a close. Everyone had already started to drift away to the adjoining room where a DJ was already in full swing.

Nick made his way in there, his gaze already searching the clusters of people for Cain's familiar back. "Let's see if you can hide from me in here."

"I'm sorry."

He turned to find an attractive blonde woman who he didn't recognize behind him. He gave her no more than a cursory glance. "I was talking to myself."

Her lips curled up at the corners, her gaze slowly perusing him and making her interest crystal clear. "Shame! I would have been up for a quick game of hide-and-seek with the right person." Nick didn't have the heart to tell her that he really wasn't interested in getting into her underwear. At least not in the way she was picturing. Now, if she wanted to loan him some, then he might be up for talking. He muttered something suitably vague and made sure that whatever direction she was headed in, he went the opposite.

Cain proved elusive until it got beyond ridiculous. Nick would catch a glimpse of him but by the time he'd managed to separate himself from the person he was speaking to and make his way over to where he'd last seen him, Cain would no longer be there. He was going to rename him The Scarlet Pimpernel. There was no longer any question in Nick's mind, Cain was actively avoiding him. It was the only explanation for Cain managing to be in exactly the places where Nick wasn't. And he was damn good at it as well. Realizing his glass was empty, Nick swiped another from the bar, sipping it while he tried to come up with a new plan of action.

"Well, are things sorted?"

He swung around to find Theo, an expectant expression on his face. "To sort things out, I'd have to be able to talk to him. To talk to him, I'd have to be able to get within five meters of him. Short of darting him with a tranquilizer gun, I'm struggling to work out how I'm supposed to do that." Exasperation leaked into his voice as he scanned the room. "Where is he?"

Theo did his own scan. "I've just been speaking to him." He lifted a hand to point in the direction of the far corner. "He was over there. I can't see him now though. He's probably gone to take a leak."

Nick grabbed his brother by the elbow and steered him into the crowd. "Right. You're going to find him and then you're going to sit on him, or do whatever it takes until he talks to me. Because I've got you hassling me and I've got him managing to slip away any time I get close to him. This is a wedding. It's supposed to be fun. At the moment all I'm doing is chasing a man who doesn't want to be caught."

Tutting, Theo nevertheless started wending his way between groups of people "God, you're like children."

Nick let out a huff. "I'm not. It's him."

"That's what a child would say." Theo came to an abrupt halt. "There. By the dance floor. Don't fuck it up and don't make a scene or Carol will kill you for ruining her big day."

The man he'd been searching high and low for was indeed by the dance floor and the best thing was that he had his back to Nick, so he couldn't see him coming. Nick couldn't help but think of a wildlife documentary as he wended his way toward him. *The prey, busy at the watering hole, doesn't spot the predator silently and stealthily making its way toward him until it's too late and there's nothing he can do about it.* Nick planted himself firmly in front of Cain. "Got you! Finally. I need to speak to you."

Cain's eyes went wide, his nostrils flaring, and for a moment it looked like he was going to make a run for it, his gaze darting left and right as if he was seeking the closest escape route. He swallowed, his throat contracting, and Nick's eyes were irrevocably drawn to the movement. How would the tanned skin taste? He had the sudden, overwhelming urge to find out.

Finally, he seemed to concede there was nowhere to run to. It didn't stop Cain from taking a step back from Nick though. "It's not really the best time, is it?" He looked back over his shoulder as if he was searching for backup from the person he'd just been speaking to. Except, whoever it had been, they'd already cleared off, so it was just the two of them.

Nick cocked an eyebrow. "No, it probably isn't. But given you wouldn't answer my calls or texts, you haven't left me with a lot of options. We should have cleared this up weeks ago. So..."

Cain's face suddenly lit up. "Carol's on her way over. Great! I haven't had a chance to speak to her yet. I need to congratulate her and Rory."

No fucking way! There was no way when it had taken hours to get to this point that Nick was letting Cain slip through his fingers again. The problem was that weddings were rife with interruptions. He just needed five minutes alone with Cain, somewhere where people wouldn't feel they could just stroll up and join in the conversation. Inspiration hit him in a flash. He grabbed Cain's arm, mentally prepared for the feel of the taut muscles beneath his fingertips this time, and dragged him in the opposite direction to Carol, who did indeed seem to be headed their way. "Let's dance."

"What!" Cain attempted to dig his heels in, but Nick's pull was stronger. He steered them toward the center of the dance floor. It was busy but not so packed that they couldn't commandeer a bit of space for themselves. Cain still seemed to be struggling with Nick's idea. "Dance. Why? How?"

"How?" Nick couldn't help but laugh as he pulled him into his arms, Cain suddenly gaining all the flexibility and grace of a mannequin, his hands hovering in mid-air as if he had no clue where he was supposed to put them. Nick grabbed them and wrapped them around his neck. Somewhere in the back of his mind, he was aware that his current actions were largely sponsored by wine, but he couldn't bring himself to care, not when Cain looked so horrified at the concept of dancing with him that it was downright amusing. "We just sway around a bit. No one's going to expect us to reenact the lift from Dirty Dancing if that's what you're worried about."

"No, I just..." Cain shook his head, whatever he'd been going to say remaining unsaid.

It was hard to believe that the man standing so stiffly in his arms made porn. That reminded him. That was probably the first point Nick needed to address. He leaned in, placing his lips close to Cain's ear just in case anyone close by might be able to hear him over the music. God, he smelt good. A mix of aftershave and something else that was just Cain. "I'm not going to tell anyone your secret, by the way. It's completely safe with me. I didn't even tell Theo. And if I came across as being an uptight prig about it, then I'm sorry. It just took me by surprise, that's all. It's not every day you discover that someone you know stars in adult films."

The tight grip around his neck loosened slightly and a ghost of a smile hovered on Cain's lips. "You're a lawyer. You're meant to be an uptight"—he paused deliberately—"prick."

"Ouch, but then I guess I deserved that." Nick pulled Cain even closer, enjoying the way they fit together, even though he knew that he wasn't supposed to. Would they fit together just as well in bed? He was beginning to think that he'd very much like to find out. Except he couldn't, right? Because there were too many things standing in their way, like the fact that Theo had made it only too clear that he wouldn't be impressed. And then, of course, there was the small matter of Nick having certain sexual predilections that Cain under no circumstances should be privy to. Sometimes, life was strange like that. It served you up a tempting morsel that you couldn't have. For a few moments, they simply swayed together, Cain's body moving with Nick now instead of fighting him. "And as for the other thing... you know, the having feelings for me."

Cain turned back into a robot, his stance once again turning rigid. He made another attempt to pull away but Nick held on fast, his brain trying to come up with the right words to make things better between them. "I don't mind." Okay, that hadn't been the right thing to say. It made it sound like he was magnanimously generous enough to allow Cain to have a crush on him. No wonder Cain's gaze was fixed on a spot on the far side of the room. He was probably trying to learn teleportation in order to transfer himself out of Nick's arms and over there. The last thing Nick wanted to do was to make things worse between them but that seemed to be exactly what he was doing. "That came out wrong. What I meant to say was..." What was it Theo had told him? Although, if he was taking relationship advice from his younger brother, he really was fucked. Except, it wasn't a relationship was it. Not in that way, anyway. He was starting to regret the alcohol clouding his brain. "I'm really flattered—"

Cain's gaze suddenly whipped to his. "But?"

Nick stared into Cain's brown eyes. He'd never noticed the mixture of colors that made up the brown before. There even seemed to be a bit of green there. They were very pretty. "What?"

Irritation flashed in the eyes that Nick seemed unable to steer his gaze away from. "This is where you're meant to list all the arguments why it... *we* could never happen. You know like you look at me as if I'm your brother because you've known me since I was a teenager, I'm not your type, you're already seeing someone, I'm too young for you. You're a lawyer, Nick. I hope your performances in court are a damn sight more convincing than this."

Nick turned them expertly to one side, swerving to avoid the thrashing limbs of a distant cousin who'd decided to ignore the fact that it was a relatively slow dance. No doubt he was hearing completely different music in his head. "I hate the fact that you've been avoiding me."

A look of indignation bloomed on Cain's face. "Of course I've been avoiding you. You were a dick and I made a complete idiot of myself at the party. I've spent the last couple of weeks wishing I could crawl into a hole and hide. The last thing I wanted to do was rehash it. I still don't. If I could have come up with a way of avoiding the wedding without Carol hating me forever, then I wouldn't even be here."

Tightening his arms around Cain's waist, Nick let his head rest on Cain's shoulder. It felt reassuringly firm beneath his chin. He smiled at the thought that Cain would make a good pillow. "I'm sorry."

There was a long silence. Long enough for Nick to start to wonder what people were making of him and Cain dancing together. Tongues were probably starting to wag. At least Theo would know he was just trying to make amends—which he'd done, right? So he should probably let go now.

Cain sighed, his shoulder jerking under Nick's chin with the action. "Apology accepted. Can we stop dancing now?"

"No." The word was out before Nick could stop himself.

"Why not?" There was no discernible tone in Cain's voice other than mild curiosity. And Nick was good at picking up on vague undercurrents. You had to be when you spent most of your day in court trying to read between the lines of what was actually being said to pick up on what they meant. And it wasn't just the criminals. It was his esteemed colleagues too. It was a good question though. Why couldn't they stop dancing? He'd achieved what he'd set out to do. Cain had said he accepted his apology and no longer seemed to hate him, if his more relaxed stance was anything to go by. They were actually dancing now, rather than Nick attempting to lug an inanimate object around the space. He turned his head slightly to the side, his nose brushing Cain's stubble as he took a deep breath in. "You smell good."

And just like that the mannequin was back again, the muscles of Cain's shoulder turning to stone beneath his cheek. Cain shifted, probably in another attempt to get away, the action causing Nick's rapidly hardening cock to press against Cain's thigh, and forcing a startled "oh" from his lips as he recognized what it was that he could feel. Nick forced himself to straighten up, their bodies still pressed together. His eyes found Cain's, the two of them staring at each other as something invisible passed between them. Cain's lips were right there. All Nick had to do was lean slightly forward and capture them. It would just be a kiss. A little tester to see how much passion was waiting to be unleashed between them. He was beginning to suspect that the answer was a lot.

Questions hammered themselves into Nick's brain in rapid succession. They'd kiss and then what? Go to bed together? Start a relationship? Because there was no way, given Cain's confession about how he felt about Nick that Nick could just use him for one night. It had to be something more. And what would this relationship look like when Nick would be keeping a huge part of himself secret for fear of seeing the same look of disgust or disappointment in Cain's eyes that he'd seen in his previous boyfriends'.

It would be doomed from the start, right? Their relationship would come to a premature end and then Cain really wouldn't talk to him. Theo would be pissed at him for making things awkward and he'd want to know what had happened. That one kiss would be the trigger to short-term gratification followed by a much longer period of pain and upset. Unless... No, he wasn't even going there. He couldn't allow himself to dream that things could be different. It was too tempting.

"Nick?" Cain's voice was full of longing, his pupils dilated, and his cock starting to stir against Nick's thigh. Cain's eyelids started to close, his lips moving inexorably closer. Nick could almost taste them, his hands fisted in the material of Cain's suit jacket. He wanted it. He wanted him. Consequences be damned. He could deal with them later.

Someone laughed loudly, momentarily breaking the spell and reminding Nick where they were. Before Cain's lips could touch his, Nick wrenched himself away, Cain's arms falling from around his neck. He just had time to catch sight of the look of absolute devastation on Cain's face before he turned away. He walked quickly with no destination in mind, refusing to look back.

He'd done the right thing.

He kept repeating it to himself. But after several minutes, he still couldn't get it to ring true.

Chapter Nine

CAIN

Cain splashed cold water on his face before lifting his head to stare at his reflection in the mirror. He'd spent the last couple of hours chatting and joking with people and pretending that everything was fine. While all the time, quiet fury had bubbled through his veins. Who the fuck did Nick think he was? It was bad enough that he'd forced him into dancing in the first place when Cain had made it clear he didn't want to. But then what had happened after that had taken it to a whole new level. Nick had looked at him with desire, had gotten an erection. They'd been seconds away from kissing. They weren't the actions of a man that didn't find Cain attractive. Quite the opposite.

And yes, the rational part of his brain might keep trying to point out that Nick had been less than sober, but he wasn't a randy teenager who couldn't keep his body under control just because there was alcohol in his system. He'd wanted Cain. His body had said it. His eyes had said it. And then he'd just walked away without so much as a word, proving that the apology he'd spouted earlier had been absolute bullshit.

To be rejected once was bad enough. But for someone to apologize for that rejection, only to turn around and do the same thing again was unforgiveable. After the EagerBoyz party, Cain had been upset. He wasn't upset now. He was vibrating with a burst of energy that begged to be released, preferably by hitting something, Nick's face at the top of the list. It didn't help that Nick had gone missing after the stunt he'd pulled. As far as Cain could work out, he'd left the party. So even if Cain had wanted to risk causing a scene, he hadn't been able to. *Fucking coward!*

He forced himself to take a couple of deep breaths, the bathroom blessedly empty apart from him, most of the guests having already gone to bed. There was no way Cain could sleep though. He was far too wound up. Whereas Nick was probably sleeping like a baby. The thought sent another surge of pure adrenaline through him, his hands curling into fists.

Mind settled on a plan of action that might just make him feel better, he dried his face with a paper towel and then headed to the hotel bar where the last remaining party guests, including the bride and groom, were having an after-party party.

Carol rose drunkenly to her feet as he approached, nearly falling over three chairs in her haste to get to him, her floral headpiece completely askew. "Here he is! You haven't paid me enough attention tonight. I am the bride, you know. Brides should be loved and adored by everyone." She attempted a little twirl, Cain grabbing her arm to hold her up when she nearly toppled over. She paused for a moment, disorientated, before managing to turn around to face him. "There you are. You hid again."

He kissed her on the cheek and then pulled her in for a hug, feeling guilty at the thought that his drama could have overshadowed her big day, even if most of it had been confined to his head. Playing hide-and-seek with Nick had still meant that he hadn't spent enough time with the people that he should have done. In retrospect, it was a shame it hadn't proved more successful. Then he could have avoided all the dance floor stuff altogether. It seemed like his initial instincts to avoid Nick entirely had been correct. Shame Nick had had to go and fucking spoil it. He forced his mind back to Carol, stepping back to hold her at arm's length. "Have I told you how gorgeous you looked today?"

She preened for a moment before her eyes narrowed. "What do you mean *looked*?" Cain reached up and straightened her headpiece before using his thumb to rub away a bit of what looked to be strawberry jam from her cheek. He also extracted a leaf from her long blonde hair that must have been there since the ceremony outside. "Sorry. Slip of the tongue. I'm just tired. You *look* gorgeous. Rory's a very lucky man."

She started to lead him back toward the table where a small group of people sat. "It could have been you, you know, if you hadn't been such a..."

"Geek?"

She waved a dismissive hand. "No, the geek never bothered me. It's kind of endearing. I was going to say gay. I had a bit of a thing for you for about a year. You never noticed because you couldn't keep your eyes off Nick."

There was an awful lot of information for Cain to process in that sentence. Firstly, the fact that it wasn't just Theo who'd been aware of his crush on Nick, and secondly, that he'd apparently done the same to Carol as Nick had done to him. "Sorry, I didn't know."

"It's fine." She made a wild grab for a bottle of champagne on the table, holding it up in the air. "You'll have a drink with us, won't you?" She giggled. "I promise to carry you to bed when the merest sniff gets you drunk." She waved a finger in the vague direction of her husband of a few hours. "Don't get jealous. Cain is more likely to sleep with you than he is me." She blinked a few times, turning her attention back to Cain. "Please don't sleep with Rory. I love him."

Cain laughed while Rory just shook his head. He was probably considering what he'd gotten himself into and reconsidering his vows of until death do us part. Cain pried Carol's fingers from his arm. "I just came to find Theo, so no drink for me." At the forlorn look on her face, he felt the need to find a compromise. "But I'm definitely joining you for the wedding breakfast tomorrow."

Carol staggered back to her seat next to Rory, seemingly mollified by Cain's assurances that she'd get to see him the next day. Besides, she was probably too drunk to remember much of their conversation the next day anyway. Happy that he hadn't caused offense, Cain turned his attention to Theo, who was looking at him expectantly after hearing his name mentioned. Cain made a "come away from the table" gesture, retreating over to the far side of the otherwise empty bar and waiting till Theo joined him there. He got straight to the point, the seething buzz under his skin that had dulled somewhat while he was talking to Carol back with a vengeance. "Do you and Nick still do that emergency thing where you give each other a spare copy of your keycards?" It was something they'd done ever since they were kids and Theo had managed to lock himself out of a hotel room in the middle of the night in nothing but a towel.

At Theo's nod, Cain held his hand out. "I need it."

EAGER FOR MORE

A look of alarm crossed Theo's face. "Whoa there! I can't give Nick's room key to just anyone. It's for emergencies and emergencies only."

Cain went with the part of the argument that he felt he had the most leeway with. "I'm not just anyone. It hurts me that you would say that. How many times have you told me that I'm like family to you?" It was underhanded to use emotional blackmail but desperate times called for desperate measures. Cain had made his mind up what he was going to do and the first step was prizing the keycard from Theo's fingers.

If he was to have any chance of sleeping that night, he needed to go and give Nick a piece of his mind. But it was odds on that if he just turned up at Nick's door, he would be ignored, leaving him even more angry with the yellowbellied son of a bitch. So, he needed to get access in order to be able to get all of those words off his chest in a place that would at least be private. For once, he'd take a leaf out of the Hackett brothers' book and use manipulation if he needed to, because in his mind the end definitely justified the means in this case.

Color bloomed in Theo's cheeks. He opened his mouth and then closed it again. "That's not fair."

Cain simply raised his eyebrows at his friend. He waggled his fingers in a clear instruction to hand over the goods. Unfortunately, Theo didn't immediately jump to do his bidding. This was going to be harder than he'd thought. Theo was supposed to be drunk and amenable. Cain wasn't giving up though. He could be pretty stubborn when he set his mind to something. "Pleeeaase." He put as much wheedling into his voice as he could. The annoying thing was that he knew if it had been anyone else apart from Nick that they were discussing, Theo would have given it up in a heartbeat. Damn, the brotherly loyalty thing!

Theo crossed his arms over his chest, his chin rising in a challenge. "What do you need it for? You sorted things out, right?"

Cain's cheeks heated, the burn of anger rising once more. "Sorted things out! Is that what it looked like?"

Theo's forehead wrinkled. "Well, yeah. I saw you, talking. Just after I'd helped my brother to find you." Theo squeezed his eyes tightly shut. "Sorry, just trying to get rid of that image from my mind. There was a strange moment where it almost looked like the two of you were indulging in some sort of weird foreplay. I was mistaken, right?"

Cain wondered how many other people had noticed how close they were on the dance floor. Hopefully no one. "Yeah, you were mistaken. Your brother..." The words came out more venomously than Cain had intended them to. He forced himself to take a steadying breath. "Well, let's just say that his so-called apology left a lot to be desired. Then he ran off and hid from me without giving me any time to say what I need to say to him."

Theo's shoulders drooped. "I really thought he was going to apologize properly. I'm so sorry. So, you want to see him to...?"

"To kill him basically. But as he's not worth the time in prison, I'll settle just for telling him what I think of him. Please, Theo. I'm not going to be able to sleep until I've taken the smug git down a peg or two." He could tell that Theo was wavering from the look on his face. He just needed to find the right thing to say to push him over the edge. "You could just tell me where the keycard is and I could take it, and then technically you haven't given it to me."

Theo stared at him for a few seconds before his gaze slowly dropped to the left pocket of his trousers. Cain lunged forward before he had time to change his mind, his fingers delving right in. Theo gave a mock shudder. "Ooh careful what you're grabbing there, tiger. I dress to the left. If you haven't turned me by now, it's not going to happen. Sorry to break it to you."

Cain forgot his anger for a moment as he laughed. "You wish. Only one thing I'm after from you, Theo Hackett, and it's this." He held the keycard up with a flourish as he started to back away. He already knew what room Nick was in. "And don't worry, I've got your back. If Nick gets pissed about it, I'll claim I pickpocketed you."

He turned away with a smile, heading straight for the lift which would take him up to the fourth floor. Now that he had a means of access, he already felt better. He started to run through what he wanted to say. And if Nick was asleep, well, the fucker could wake up and listen to what he wanted to say. *Listen, Nick, you keep hurting me.* No, too needy. Better not to let the idiot know that he'd affected Cain that strongly. *I just wanted to thank you. I did have a crush on you but you being such an absolute and complete prize wanker has cured me of that. Now, I know what you're really like, I can move on to men who don't cock-tease and know what the hell they bloody want from one minute to the next. So, yeah, thank you for making me see the error of my ways. I appreciate it.* He smiled at the mirror, his own face smiling back. Yeah, that was much better. Nicholas Hackett could go to hell. Cain didn't care anymore what Nick did and with whom. After all, he was easy enough to avoid. Their paths had barely crossed for the last couple of months, and that was when Cain had been trying to see him. So if he was trying to avoid him, it stood to reason that it would be child's play.

The lift stopped and Cain made his way along the corridor until he reached the right door. He extracted the keycard from his pocket and hesitated for a moment. Should he try knocking first? There was always the chance, no matter how slim, that Nick might answer the door and not close it in his face. But then why give him the opportunity when he already had a means of access that he'd worked so hard for? He pressed the keycard against the reader until the light turned green and the door unlocked. Good old Theo! It had crossed his mind that Theo could have fobbed him off with his own keycard, but obviously he hadn't.

Pushing the door open, Cain stepped inside to find the room lit with a lamp and the bed empty. It was still made, so it wasn't a case of Nick having been asleep and then waking up, which begged the question of where he was. Cain jumped as the door clicked shut behind him, doubt starting to take hold for the first time about whether he should really be in there uninvited.

The bathroom door was ajar but Cain couldn't hear the shower running. It was the only place that Nick could be though, right? Unless he wasn't there at all? Maybe he'd hooked up with someone at the wedding and gone back to their room. The thought gave fuel to the white-hot flame of fury and it started to grow again, despite Cain having only told himself minutes earlier that he didn't give a fuck what Nick did. He guessed it took longer than that to get over a crush that had spanned ten years.

The fresh injection of anger was enough to have his feet moving toward the bathroom. Cain needed to know one way or the other. If Nick was there, well, then he'd get a chance to say everything he'd practiced. And if he wasn't there, he could have the satisfaction of knowing that he was an even bigger dick than he'd thought for rubbing up against him and then hooking up with someone else.

The light was on in the bathroom meaning that Cain had a fully unobstructed view of what he found there, which was Nick. Almost naked. Normally, it would have been those parts that drew his interest. But it was hard to concentrate on them when the only covering Nick wore was a tiny pair of lacy blue panties which barely contained the erection he sported.

Cain sagged against the doorway, his brain short-circuiting, and all the things he'd planned on saying disappearing into the ether. He said the only words he could force out of his mouth: "Fucking hell!"

Chapter Ten

NICK

There was no getting around it after what had happened on the dance floor. Nick was a prize asshole. Possibly the biggest asshole ever to have walked the planet. He'd completely ruined his apology, rendering it absolutely worthless by getting aroused, nearly kissing Cain, and then running off. There was no point in trying to lie to himself anymore. He was attracted to Cain. Not just a little bit attracted, but a hell of a lot. If it was just a case of the wedding, he might have been able to put it down to too much wine. But what about the party? What about when he hadn't realized it was Cain standing with his back to him? He'd been virtually drooling over him and planning to throw himself at him.

In a dazed state of confusion, Nick had decided that the best course of action was to leave the reception. Carol was family but they'd never been that close. Not like she and Theo were. Probably something to do with there being less of a difference in age between Theo and Carol. It was doubtful she'd notice his absence, and if she did, he could always plead illness. Insanity would be more truthful but it was close enough.

Back in his hotel room, he hadn't known what to do with himself. He kept revisiting that moment on the dance floor, remembering how close he'd come to kissing Cain in front of everyone, kept recalling how Cain had felt in his arms, all hard muscle, hot skin, and eyes that said "yes, please." He'd seen that muscle first-hand when he'd dealt with a shirtless Cain at the party and remembering that didn't help either.

With a cock desperate for release, he'd found himself in front of his suitcase, the usual battle starting up. *Seriously, can't you even have a wank without playing dress up? What kind of man does that make you?* He didn't even know why he'd brought them. Had it really reached the point where he couldn't even attend a bloody family wedding without tucking women's underwear away in the bottom of his suitcase? But it was like a compulsion, he just couldn't stop. It was almost like the more he tried not to do it, the more he needed it. So hidden away in a secret compartment at the bottom of his case were three pairs of panties—a tantalizing mixture of lace and satin designed to appeal, no matter what mood he might find himself in.

He crouched down, his fingers delving into the compartment until he could feel the cold slide of the satin against his knuckles, a strange mixture of both calm and arousal coursing through him. He didn't want satin tonight, though. He craved the scratchiness of lace against his balls. He pulled them out, and within five minutes they were snugly encasing his erection.

The mirror in the bathroom was better than the one in the bedroom, so he went in there. Besides, it felt better to have two doors between himself and the rest of the hotel guests.

Once in there, he closed his eyes, doing what he always did, letting the arousal slowly ramp up before he gave in to touching himself. Even then he started by only allowing himself the occasional brush of his fingertips over his fabric-covered cock, just enough to tease but not enough to ease any of the burning desire throbbing in his balls and cock. He couldn't have said what it was that had made him open his eyes. Maybe there'd been a slight noise, or perhaps it was just that he'd somehow been able to tell that someone was there.

All he knew was that when he did open them, he found himself staring straight into Cain's shocked face. Except, he couldn't be. It made no sense. The hotel room door had been locked. Nick knew it was; he'd checked it. What did that mean? Was he hallucinating? Had he slipped and banged his head and this was all part of some strangely lucid dream? God, he hoped so. That way he'd be able to wake up. With that in mind, he tried squeezing his eyes shut. Unfortunately, Cain was still there when he opened them, his gaze locked on Nick's crotch. So much for that theory.

Nick was existing in some sort of frozen stillness. He had no idea what to do. No idea what to say. Time stretched between them never-ending, the words that finally spilled from Cain's lips exhibiting the same shock as his face did. "Fucking hell!"

At least the epithet had Nick's frozen limbs moving again. He made a clumsy grab for a towel, relieved when the soft material met his fingers at the first attempt. He kept his gaze fixed on the floor, his cheeks burning while he wrapped it around his waist. The damage was already done though, right? There was no coming up with any sort of excuse that would work. There was only facing up to the aftermath and maybe limiting the damage if he could work out how.

He continued to stare at the floor, unable to bring himself to look at Cain. He needed to say something. But, what? "It's not what it looks like." The silence that followed his statement didn't help matters. Why wasn't Cain saying anything? He'd prefer him to call him a pervert, rather than this... nothing. Now that he was over the initial shock, a sick realization was starting to sink in. Cain knew his secret. Cain would tell Theo, and then his own brother would never look at him the same way again. And still the goddamn silence.

"So fucking hot!"

Nick's head whipped up to stare at Cain, wondering if his ears were deceiving him, or whether Cain was simply mocking him. But the only emotion present on Cain's face was pure lust. Lust directed at him.

Before he could even begin to comprehend what the hell was going on, Cain was stepping closer, his fingers grazing the edge of Nick's towel, and a note of pleading in his voice. "Take it off, please. I want to see."

"I don't... I can't..." Nick didn't have a clue how he'd intended to end either of those sentences. He needed to reach out and loosen Cain's grip on the towel, needed to unfurl his fingers before Cain got any ideas in his head about taking matters into his own hands. But he didn't seem to have any control over his limbs. At least that's the only excuse he could come up with for the fact that when Cain tugged gently, he did absolutely nothing to stop him.

They both watched the towel flutter to the floor. And then Nick was exposed to Cain's gaze. There was nothing to hide the fact that he was standing there dressed in only a tiny pair of lacy blue panties. You would think, given the shock, that his cock would have had the good sense to settle down, but if anything he was even harder, the head peeping over the waistband as if it was desperate to say hello to Cain.

Nick could barely breathe as Cain returned to staring at his crotch. Where was the disgust he'd expected to see? The loathing in Cain's eyes? He could see neither. Only twin flags of color in his cheeks and a burning desire in his eyes. What did that mean? That his feelings for Nick were strong enough that he didn't care? Or did he actually like it?

Nick should probably have been asking some of the questions aloud rather than engaging in an internal debate, but that would mean being able to formulate a sentence, and the possibility of needing to brace himself for answers he didn't want to hear. So instead he simply stood there, so still he may as well have been a statue in a museum.

Cain finally raised his head, his heated gaze taking its own sweet time to trail slowly up Nick's heaving chest before reaching his face. He braced himself for the questions to start. *How long? How did it start? What else do you like to wear? How does it make you feel?* He'd heard them all before, had tackled the common assumption that people who wore women's underwear wanted to go the whole hog and graduate to stockings and suspenders. Or that he wanted to spend his weekends performing as a drag queen. None of those things were true.

Nick tensed as Cain narrowed the space between them, their chests almost touching. There was no curiosity in the familiar brown eyes, surprisingly. Cain gave a wry smile. "Do you know why I came here, Nick?"

He shook his head, unable to tear his eyes away from Cain's face. He swallowed, attempting to force some saliva into his mouth and find his voice again. "No idea."

The expression on Cain's face was incredulous. "Really? You get hard when you're dancing with me, you look at me the way you did, and then you run away *again*, and you think I'll be okay with that? Twice I've tried to kiss you and twice you've rejected me."

Nick winced. "It's complicated."

Cain's glance flicked back to Nick's crotch for the briefest moment before returning to his face. "Yeah, I'm beginning to see that." He let out a weary sigh. "I was supposed to tell you that you being an absolute dick has cured me of the stupid crush I had on you. Only..." He shook his head, whatever words he'd been going to say dying on his lips. "I am such a fucking idiot."

If Nick was supposed to be able to make sense of what Cain was saying, he was failing miserably. They seemed more like verbalized thoughts. Thoughts he couldn't follow. "I don't see why you're an idiot. You haven't done anything."

"No, but I'm about to." Brown eyes fastened on Nick's, a smile playing on Cain's lips. "What is it they say—third time lucky."

Nick barely had time to process the words, never mind make a connection before he was crowded back against the bathroom wall, the heat of Cain's body through his thin shirt burning Nick's bare chest. He just had time to release a groan at the feel of Cain's crotch pressing against his lace-clad cock before lips descended on his. Right. Third time lucky kissing him. Hands curled around his ass, cupping it through the panties, lips moving insistently over his.

Nick tried to remember why this was such a bad idea. Something about Theo. That was it; he wouldn't be happy. Theo wasn't here though. What else? He'd known Cain for years ever since he was a teenager. So what? That just made them friends. Sleeping with friends rather than a stranger was good, right? There was already trust there and a mutual respect. You didn't need to get to know them. You could dispense with all that initial awkwardness.

He spread his hands over Cain's chest fully intending on pushing him away. Only his hands were operating on an entirely different scheme to his brain. They moved over the thin fabric of their own accord, tracing over the dips and hollows of the chest he'd already seen was in perfect physical condition. He hated the material being there. He wanted it bare, nothing but warm skin beneath his fingertips.

Cain lifted his head, his face twisted in anguish. "Nick, kiss me back, please. Don't torture me like this."

Who could resist a plea like that? Not Nick, that was for sure. Or maybe he was down to his last shred of resistance as it was—hard muscles, body heat, and grasping hands rendering him a throbbing ball of desire. This wasn't Cain, friend of his brother and the fourteen-year-old who'd trailed around after him like a lost puppy; this was Cain, the hot and sexy man who was all grown up and more.

He twisted them around so that Cain's back met the wall before slamming his lips down on his. There was a moment of frozen surprise from the younger man before he melted, mouth opening and tongue coming out to tangle with Nick's. Nick sank his fingers into Cain's hair holding his head still while he tasted and explored to his heart's content. His fingers plucked at Cain's shirt, still yearning for that bare skin, but not enough to release his mouth in order to achieve it.

In the end, it was Cain who paused for breath first, blown pupils meeting Nick's own gaze, which was no doubt just as dazed. "You kissed me back."

As obvious statements went, it should have won a prize, Nick smiling despite his best attempts to hold it back. He didn't bother responding. He had more important things to think about, like the opportunity now that they weren't kissing to set to work on the buttons on Cain's shirt. His fingers were strangely uncooperative, the simple task of trying to thread the button back through the hole taking far longer than it should have done. Finally, after what felt like hours, he released the last one, peeling back the two halves of the shirt to reveal the sculpted chest beneath. It really was a work of art. How had Nick never noticed what was lurking under Cain's clothes? He was a lawyer. He was meant to be observant. Yet, somehow the hottest fucking guy he'd met for ages had been right under his nose, and not just under his nose but lusting after him.

"I never thought you'd look at me like that."

Nick was so lost in thought that it took a moment for the quietly spoken words to register. It took all the willpower he had to tear his eyes away from the bronzed expanse of chest in order to meet Cain's gaze. Brutal honesty spilled from Nick's mouth before he could stop it. "Neither did I." He trailed his fingers down the chest he'd been so desperate to touch, a new target already in mind. The button of Cain's trousers gave way much more easily than his shirt buttons had. Nick eased the zipper down slowly over the bulge straining at the material, Cain sucking in a breath as the back of Nick's fingers grazed his cock.

A quick glance upward confirmed that Cain was completely on board with where this was going, so Nick carried on, his fingers encircling the stiff column of flesh he found there. He squeezed gently, enraptured by the moan that burst forth from Cain's lips. Nick dropped to his knees, his nose replacing his fingers as he nuzzled the rigid flesh and breathed in the musky scent. It elicited another breathy moan from Cain. He could have listened to them all day—the sound addictive in the best possible way.

"Nick, please."

A part of him wanted to prolong the agony and keep teasing Cain, but he'd be torturing himself as well. Nick slowly peeled down the fabric of Cain's briefs to reveal his reward, the stiff cock that sprung out almost hitting him in the face. He took a moment to admire it. As cocks went, it was pretty—good-sized with only a slight curve. No wonder Cain did porn. He was gorgeous from head to toe, every single muscular inch of him. His hand fastened around the base of Cain's cock, holding it in position.

He licked his lips, desperate to taste but holding off for just a few more seconds to give them both a chance to savor the anticipation. Cain was silent save for his ragged breathing. Nick lowered his head slowly, his lips sliding over the head, the fit so perfect that the two things could have been made for each other. He hadn't given a blow job for ages, and God he'd missed it. Nothing beat that sensation of taking cock deep while trying to avoid tumbling over the edge to where imminent choking was inevitable. He let Cain's cock nudge the back of his throat before lifting off, his head tipping back to make eye contact. Only Cain's eyes were closed, an expression akin to pain on his face.

Nick was transfixed. He'd known Cain was horny. It was hard not to be aware when the evidence of that was lodged down your throat, but Cain looked as if he was fighting the urge to come after only a couple of minutes.

At the lack of contact, Cain's eyelashes fluttered, his eyes opening a few seconds later. "Don't stop!"

"I want you to watch." Nick had no idea why that was so important to him, only that it was. Maybe he needed to see the look of adoration in Cain's eyes that he couldn't quite manage to hide. Nick had done nothing to earn it. Quite the opposite in fact, but he'd be greedy and take it anyway.

Cain nodded, and Nick went back to work. This time he got to look into Cain's eyes as he sucked his cock, got to read every little micro expression that flitted across his face. Only when Cain's hands were fisted in his hair and his body taut with the desperate desire not to come, did Nick stop. They weren't done yet. Not by a long chalk. There were plenty more things he wanted to experience first. But not squashed in the bathroom. It was about time they moved to the bedroom. He wanted to lay Cain out on the bed where they could both be more comfortable and... well, do all sorts of things to him. The list was endless.

He stood, only remembering what he wore when Cain's gaze immediately dropped to his crotch, his nostrils flaring. Nick faltered, his fingers slipping into the waistband. "I'll take them off."

"Don't you dare."

The words were almost spat at Nick. There was no doubting the veracity of Cain's response. He dropped his hands. "You really like them?"

Cain stalked forward, his jaw set stubbornly as if he was worried Nick was going to argue with him. "Are you fucking kidding me? I love them. On you, anyway." His gaze skirted over Nick's body. "All that muscle and then they're so feminine." He smiled. "I didn't know I liked it until today. But yeah, I need you to leave them on. I love the way your cock looks wrapped in lace."

For a second, Nick felt like all his Christmases had come at once. Then one of the words Cain had used sank in—*feminine*. Alarm bells started to ring. He'd been here before and it had never ended well. He lifted his chin, meeting Cain's gaze head on. "If you're expecting me to act like a girl, you're in for a bit of a shock." He waved a hand down at his lace-covered cock. "Just because this turns me on doesn't mean I want to be a woman. I like to top."

Cain stared at him for a moment with his mouth hanging open. Then to Nick's surprise he started laughing. "Great! That should be perfect, then, because I prefer to bottom." He lunged forward stealing a kiss from Nick's lips. "I want you to fuck me wearing them." Cain paused, a question in his eyes that he eventually voiced. "If that's alright with you?"

The feeling that hit Nick was akin to walking into an inferno, his whole body suddenly blisteringly hot. It was more than alright. It was more than he could ever have hoped for. And who'd have thought that it would come from Cain of all people. He guessed in a way it made sense. Cain made porn. Therefore, it stood to reason that he'd have less hang-ups than the average person, but still... He nodded, surging forward, and capturing Cain's lips again, the two of them managing to maintain contact as they maneuvered themselves out of the bathroom and over to the double bed.

Nick scrambled backwards on the bed. The thought that they shouldn't be doing this hadn't gone away completely, but it had subsided to no more than a slight niggle at the back of his head. One that was easy enough to dismiss. After all, they were two adults. It was entirely up to them what they did. No one else's business. Cain parted Nick's thighs, crawling onto the bed and fitting his body in the space between them, his gaze firmly fixed on the junction of Nick's thighs barely covered by the blue lace. The initial heat he'd seen in Cain's eyes hadn't faded. If anything, it had grown. Cain was looking at Nick as if Nick's cock was a precious treasure he couldn't wait to get his hands—or mouth—on.

Nick tensed as Cain's fingers started to explore, barely grazing the edges of the lace to start with. Then they got bolder, moving to follow the folds of material, but only with the slightest pressure. Nick squirmed, needing more, needing... something. He watched Cain's face, the other man's lips curving into a smile as he traced the shape of Nick's cock through the lace. Then a warm, hot mouth was touching him instead of fingers, Nick arching up as a gasp tore out of his throat. It was quickly followed by several more as Cain refused to let up, the lace growing damper and damper beneath his oral ministrations, Nick's cock throbbing fit to burst.

When Cain's mouth finally closed around the head of Nick's cock, it was all he could do not to start crying. It was too intense, too special, too everything. It wasn't just about the pure, physical sensation. It was about Cain taking the time to show him that not only did Nick's penchant for wearing women's underwear not bother him, but that he liked it. He really liked it. No one would spend so long on that one area just out of generosity. No one would wear the same expression that Cain did, like they were a drowning man being offered a lifeline.

Nick leaned up onto his elbows, needing to watch and immortalize the moment. Cain held his gaze as his tongue—yet again—swiped across the material, the visual and the sensation combining to push Nick even closer to the edge. In fact, so close that if he didn't do something about it, he was going to come without even getting his cock out. He pushed his hand into Cain's thick, luxurious hair, using the grip to halt his movement. "I'm going to come if you don't stop."

Cain dipped his head again, giving Nick another one of those dizzying licks along the length of his still covered cock. "So, come. I want to see it. Just think how hot it'll look." He raised his head, grinning wickedly. "Lace and cum."

It was all Nick could do not to come right there and then and make Cain's words come true. His fingernails dug into his palms as he fought for control. He pushed up, catching Cain enough off balance that he could free himself and reverse their positions. It left Cain on his back with Nick straddling him. He grabbed Cain's arms, pinning them to the bed as he sat astride him, his cock throbbing for release. "Fucking hell! You are trouble."

Cain's grin didn't hold even a shred of guilt. He made no attempt to free his arms, both of them knowing that given Cain's superior physique he could have done so in a heartbeat. "You're a lawyer. You're supposed to be good at dealing with trouble."

"Unfortunately, I can't send you to prison for nearly making me come." Nick couldn't stop himself from running his hands over the bulging muscles of Cain's biceps as he spoke, his skin like warm silk beneath his fingertips.

"Guess you'll have to come up with a different way of dealing with me, then."

Now calm enough that he could risk it, Nick let go of Cain's arms, his fingers grazing the stubble on Cain's face. Cain was all interesting sensations and textures. The years where he'd missed out on touching him suddenly seemed like such a waste. "I've got a good idea but you're overdressed."

They both focused on Cain's trousers, unzipped from Nick blowing him earlier, but still very much present. Cain's eyes crinkled. "Easily solved. Why don't I fix that right now, and while I do you can sort out the stuff we're going to need?"

It was a symptom of just how much Nick's brain was laboring to process anything beneath the haze of lust that it took him so long to work out that "stuff" constituted condoms and lube. He scrambled off the bed, struggling to get his bearings. Had he even brought any? It wasn't like he'd been expecting to hook up at a family wedding. He was vaguely aware of rustling in the background as Cain stripped. Spying his wallet on top of the chest of drawers, he rushed over to it, praying that he'd find a condom and lube in it. His fingers fumbled to open it in order to gain access. Christ! It was like the shirt buttons all over again.

"Nick?"

The request was husky and full of so much longing that it almost made Nick drop the condom he'd finally managed to locate. Grabbing a packet of lube, he dropped his wallet on the floor before turning back to the bed, oxygen freezing in his lungs at the alluring sight. A naked Cain was laid out on the bed, his feet planted on the mattress so that nothing was left to the imagination. Every tanned, muscular inch. Nick's gaze was irrevocably drawn to the shadowed cleft between Cain's thighs, the puckered hole on display almost begging him to bury his cock deep inside it.

Cain watched Nick's every move as he ripped the condom packet open with his teeth, his chest rising and falling rapidly and a delicious flush coating his chest. A look of panic crossed Cain's face as Nick's hands drifted closer to his crotch. "Leave them on!"

Nick smiled. He had absolutely no intention of taking them off. What were the chances of him meeting someone else who'd beg him to fuck them wearing lace? His subconscious said slim to none, so he wasn't missing this chance for the world. He shrugged off the negative thoughts. Now wasn't the time. Tonight was about enjoying the rare gift he'd been given, not worrying about what came later. That was a problem for tomorrow.

He pulled the panties down enough that his cock sprang free but his balls remained encased in the lace. He avoided looking at Cain as he rolled the condom down his length and applied lube; there was only so much stimulation he could handle at one time. Then there was nothing left to do but climb on the bed, Cain's muscular thighs brushing his hips as he eased himself between them. Nick's arms shook as he held himself still above Cain, fighting the urge to push his cock straight into him. "What do you need?" His tongue felt thick, the words difficult to get out.

Cain shook his head. "Nothing. Just you."

"Are you sure?" An emphatic nod met his inquiry. That was a huge relief. Nick wasn't sure he could have waited any longer anyway, not with his body one huge throbbing nerve begging to be satisfied. It felt like he'd been staving off orgasm for hours. The heat of Cain's stare burned into him as he carefully lined up his cock. It crossed his mind that in a few seconds there would be no going back. But it was already too late, Cain's body opening to him and the delicious warmth on the head of his cock encouraging him deeper.

There was a moment of resistance, the tension in Cain's body making Nick freeze. His gaze flicked to Cain's face, ready to withdraw, ready to apologize, but then in a heartbeat it was gone, Cain's expression one of reassurance as his hands moved to Nick's hips, encouraging him to move.

Nick didn't need asking twice, sealing his lips over Cain's as he thrust into him. He swallowed every gasp that came from Cain's lips, delighting in the fact that he was responsible for them.

Lasting a long time was never an option, not with the constant scratch of the lace over his sensitive balls, coupled with the tight grip of Cain's ass around his cock. All he could do was try and concentrate on making it as good as possible for the short time it would last. Sucking on Cain's tongue, he moved his hips faster and pushed his cock deeper, Cain's hips rising to meet his, giving as good as he was getting. They were so perfectly synchronized, so perfectly matched that Nick found it hard to believe that this was the first time between them.

His balls already tightening with the first tingles of orgasm, Nick struggled to hold on, to make the delicious ecstasy last just that few seconds longer. But when Cain's hands moved down his back, grasping his ass and pushing the lace against Nick's hole, he was lost, his body jerking as he thrust deep and spilled himself into the condom. Riding his own orgasm, limbs still switching, Nick was dimly aware of Cain jerking himself off, and his throaty groan as he came.

It took a few minutes before Nick could gather himself enough to withdraw from Cain and get rid of the condom. He tumbled back against the pillows, exhausted. There were a million things they needed to talk about, a million things Nick needed to say to Cain that were important. But as sleep dragged him into its embrace, he had to concede that they'd have to wait until tomorrow.

Chapter Eleven

CAIN

Cain turned his head into the pillow, burying his face in the cotton. As consciousness started to work its way through his body, he couldn't shake the feeling that something wasn't right. His head was fine, so it wasn't that he'd drunk too much. In fact, he'd avoided alcohol altogether at the wedding, the evening at the party where he'd confessed his feelings to Nick while under the influence still too raw. *Nick!* His eyes shot open, staring at the blond head that lay on the pillow next to his.

Everything came back to him in a rush: the dance floor, getting the keycard from Theo, the plan to tear a strip off Nick, and all of that disintegrating into nothing at the discovery of Nick wearing nothing but a skimpy pair of panties. Nick, of all people. It was a running joke between himself and Theo about how straitlaced his brother was. Well, he hadn't been straitlaced last night. Far from it. He'd been a world away from the uptight lawyer when he'd fucked Cain. That last memory hovered in Cain's brain like the best sort of hallucination. Except it wasn't a hallucination.

They'd fucked and it had been fantastic. The evidence was in the man sleeping next to him, and the slight twinge in Cain's ass as he shifted position. Nick had fucked him. He'd been fucked by Nick; the man he'd lusted after for years. There weren't words for how it made Cain feel.

Nick was still asleep, his breathing deep and even. It was probably a good thing; the way Cain was staring at him, he probably would have freaked him out, had he been awake. Cain concentrated on recalling every single moment of the previous night from the moment he'd stepped into the bathroom. Nick had almost seemed scared at first, as if he'd expected Cain to mock him.

The thought had never crossed Cain's mind, not when his hands had been itching to touch and feel, to find out what that lace would feel like with the added bonus of Nick's bare skin beneath it. And it *had* felt great. Beneath his fingers, beneath his tongue, rubbing against him while Nick had fucked him. Yeah, Cain was definitely a convert to the previously unknown delights of a man in women's underwear. At least when the person inside them was Nick, anyway.

He shifted his head closer to Nick's. How would he react when he woke and saw Cain there? Would he smile at the memory of what they'd done together? Or would there be regret there that would slice Cain's heart to ribbons? He guessed that he wouldn't have to wait too long to find out. Cain lifted the cover, his lips quirking at the sight of the scrap of blue lace that Nick still wore. Had he worn them under his wedding suit? It was doubtful. Given the look on Nick's face when Cain had walked in on him, he couldn't imagine him being that brave. His fingers itched to reach out and touch, to explore the body that had been all his, the previous night. He swallowed the urge, not wanting Nick to wake to Cain groping him. He propped himself up on one elbow. He could quite happily spend all day looking at Nick.

A familiar ringtone cut into those thoughts—his. The only question was where his phone was. He scrambled out of bed, tracking the noise to his discarded trousers. Fumbling in the pocket, he pulled his phone out. Given it was probably about three seconds from going to voicemail, he answered it without checking the caller ID.

"Morning, sunshine. Thought you were ignoring me there for a minute."

Theo! *Fuck!* His gaze automatically shot to Nick, but, somehow, he'd managed to remain sleeping all through the insistent ringtone and Cain's undignified departure from the bed. He covered the speaker of the phone with his hand, hissing out an urgent request for assistance. "Nick?" No response. Not even a slight stir. Cain put the phone back to his ear. "Erm... hi. Morning. Not ignoring you, I wouldn't do that. Unless you'd done something, which you haven't. Not that I know of." He was rambling. He forced himself to stop talking. Standing naked in Nick's room, the last thing he needed was a suspicious Theo. He lifted a foot, giving Nick's sleeping figure a firm nudge. Still no response. The man slept like he was in a coma.

"Were you still asleep?"

"Erm... yeah. It was a late night."

Theo snorted. "I'm just getting dressed and then I'll come to your room. You promised Carol you'd attend the wedding breakfast."

Cain checked his watch. Fuck! It was nearly nine, which was the time it was due to start. "Don't do that!" The words were out before he could stop them. Great! The more he tried not to be suspicious, the more suspicious he managed to sound. He wasn't cut out for this morning-after subterfuge. With one hand, he started to gather up the remainder of his clothes, the phone still pressed to his ear.

"Why?"

Good question. Why couldn't Theo come to his room, apart from the truth, of course, which was that he wasn't in it, so Theo wouldn't find him there. "I can meet you in the breakfast room. You don't need to go out of your way."

"Dude! I'm a couple of floors above you. It's not like I need to call a cab." Theo yawned loudly. "I'll see you in five minutes."

Cain was left listening to dead air as Theo ended the call. "Fuck! Fuck! Fuck!" He began pulling his clothes on at record speed. "Nick?" At least this time, he stirred slightly. Cain repeated his name more loudly, Nick letting out a small murmur, his eyes still closed. Finally. "I have to go. Theo's on his way to my room. If he gets there and I'm not there, then he's going to put two and two together about where I spent the night. I'm assuming you're not keen on your brother finding out about us like this?"

If Nick answered, Cain didn't hear him, he was too busy letting himself out of the door. There were more things to think about than just Theo. Even being seen in the same clothes as the previous night would set off the rumor mill. The last thing he wanted was to find himself the subject of speculation at breakfast. Because then what would he do? Lie? That meant he needed to make it down three floors without being seen. Not an easy thing to achieve when Carol and Rory's wedding guests made up a large majority of the hotel's clientele. And Theo could already be on his way to his room, which didn't leave a lot of time to be careful.

He bypassed the lift, heading straight for the stairs, figuring that with all the sore heads there would be this morning, there was going to be a lot less chance of bumping into people on the stairs. He felt like a criminal as he made his way down them, two stairs at a time while listening out for the sound of familiar voices.

He was feeling better by the time he got to his floor without having seen or heard a single soul. His hotel room was fairly close to the stairwell, so once he stepped into the corridor he'd only have a few meters to go. He'd taken one step, his room tantalizingly close when a pair of familiar voices drifted down the corridor from just around the bend. Oh, for fuck's sake! Theo and Nick's parents. He dived back into the stairwell, pressing his back against the wall, and praying they were taking the lift. The voices came closer before fading away again as they walked straight past.

Cain's breath left his lungs in a rush. He counted to thirty, not daring to wait any longer when five minutes had to be nearly up. On thirty, he cautiously stuck his head out. At sighting the empty corridor, he made a run for it, his keycard already in his hand. He skidded to a halt in front of the door and pressed the card against the door panel.

Nothing happened.

He tried again. Same result. What the hell! He did a few calculations in his head, concluding that it was definitely the right floor *and* the right room. So why wasn't it opening? Major panic set in until he realized what an idiot he was. Reaching into his pocket, he pulled out the other keycard, the one that opened *his* room, rather than Nick's, and pressed that to the sensor. The green light lit up immediately, the door clicking open. He almost fell inside, slumping against the wall in relief.

It lasted all of two seconds as a knock sounded on the door, a familiar voice not waiting for it to be opened. "Hey! Your hot date for breakfast is here, you lucky boy. You ready?" The door handle rattled. "Let me in."

That had been far too close and he wasn't out of the woods yet. Cain was a blur of motion as he stripped off the clothes he'd only put on a few minutes ago. "One minute!" Running into the bathroom, he threw his clothes in a corner before shoving his arms into a hotel robe. Belting the robe, he rushed to the door and flung it open, a huge smile pasted on his face. "Morning."

Theo stared at him suspiciously. "Why are you out of breath? And why is your robe inside out?"

Cain glanced down. *Fuck!* He reminded himself that Theo knew nothing. There was no way he could. He hadn't had time to visit Nick's room, so there was no way he could have spoken to him. Besides, Nick was hardly likely to spill the fact that the two of them had had sex. Mind-blowing unforgettably fantastic sex. Cain reminded himself that now really wasn't the time to be taking a trip down memory lane, particularly with Theo continuing to subject him to a narrow-eyed stare. "I was just about to get in the shower." He gestured down at his body. "I figured you wouldn't want me opening the door naked. I didn't realize that you expected me to be the height of sartorial elegance first thing in the morning."

He moved aside as Theo pushed past him to gain access to the room. Cain's heart thudded as Theo's gaze swept the room, as if he expected to find something of note. It was stupid to be so nervous. Now, if they'd been in Nick's room, Detective Theo might have found something. But nothing had happened here, so there was nothing to find. No discarded condoms. No sleeping man in his bed.

"Dude, why have you made your bed? You're in a hotel. They're only going to change the sheets once you've checked out anyway. Part of the fun of staying in a hotel is the fact that you've got people to clean up after you."

Cain followed Theo's gaze to the perfectly made-up bed that looked like no one had slept in it, because of course he hadn't: he'd been in Nick's. He shrugged, hoping that the sweat he could feel breaking out on his upper lip wasn't obvious. "I don't know. Force of habit, I guess."

He waited, watching Theo's face as his friend only grunted before lowering himself to sit on the end of the bed, his head tipping back to meet Cain's gaze. "So, what happened last night?"

"Last night?" Cain reached up to rub the back of his neck. "What do you mean?"

Theo rolled his eyes. "Did you make him grovel?"

"Him?"

Theo looked at him as if he was an imbecile. "What's with you this morning? I'd think you were hungover if it wasn't for the fact you didn't drink anything. Now, Nick's going to be hungover that's for sure, given the amount of Prosecco he got through yesterday. And Nick's the *him* I'm referring to, spaghetti brains. Remember? You were all set to go and give him a piece of your mind. So, yeah, what happened?"

Various responses flashed through Cain's head. In the end, he settled for the safest. The one that had him absolutely nowhere near Nick's room. "Oh, I decided not to go and see him in the end. I was probably just being oversensitive." He couldn't get something Theo had said out of his head though. "Do you think Nick was drunk yesterday?"

Theo leaned back on his elbows, not bothering to give the question much consideration. "God, yeah. I was relieved that he left when he did. I was worried he was going to end up in bed with someone he shouldn't. There was a blonde woman who could barely take her eyes off him." He started laughing and Cain forced himself to join in with it, even as his heart sank and he started replaying snippets of the previous night, searching for any signs that Nick had been too drunk to make a rational decision. He hadn't seemed drunk though. It would kill him if Nick had only slept with him under the influence of alcohol.

Oblivious to the turmoil going on inside Cain, Theo yawned before checking his watch. He gestured to the bathroom door that Cain had left open. "You better get a move on if you still need to shower." He lay back on the bed, making himself comfortable. "I'll wait and then we can go down to the big, posh breakfast together."

Cain didn't want breakfast. He didn't want anything but reassurance that Nick had been fully in charge of his faculties when they'd had sex. But as he wasn't going to get that from Nick's younger brother, he guessed that he had no choice but to put a smile on his face and go and shower.

THE TABLE WAS LOVELY. The breakfast was to die for, and even those people who'd been up late the night before, including Carol and Rory, were in fine form. But Cain was too lost in thought to be able to appreciate any of it. He toyed with the food on his plate while he ran through every scrap of evidence he could come up with. Nick hadn't been slurring his words, but then there hadn't been a great deal of talking, so that wasn't conclusive. He hadn't tasted of alcohol, and Cain should know, after all, he'd had his tongue in his mouth for long enough that he should have been able to tell. Nothing pointed toward him having been drunk. He could have sobered up, right?

"Where's Nick?"

Cain lifted his head at the mention of the very man he'd been thinking about, Carol directing the question at Theo, who sat on Cain's right-hand side.

Theo chewed and swallowed his mouthful of scrambled eggs before answering, his nose wrinkling. "Knowing him, probably on his phone answering some urgent lawyer-type question that can't wait until he's back in the office. Either that or talking to Bailey. The two of them have this weird thing where they like to speak to each other first thing in the morning. It's positively nauseating."

"Are they a couple?"

It took all the willpower Cain had, not to glare at Lily, the person who'd asked the additional question. He continued to play with his food, pretending a complete lack of interest in the answer, his pulse picking up. Nick had said they weren't together, had laughed when Cain had suggested it, but then that didn't mean he'd been telling the truth. Relationships could be complicated. It was always possible that he and Bailey had some sort of on/off thing going on, meaning that when Cain had asked weeks ago, he'd technically been telling the truth. Great! Now he'd not only slept with Nick in that scenario, but he'd helped him to cheat. Would Nick do that? *Maybe if he was drunk.*

Theo cleared his throat. "I think..." Whatever insight he'd been about to offer was lost as he suddenly changed tack. "Oh, there he is. You can ask him yourself."

Cain's head whipped up so fast, it was a wonder he didn't do himself an injury, his heart immediately launching into a rhythm better befitting someone halfway through a marathon. And there Nick was, in all his blond glory. The black jeans and cream jumper he wore, a far cry from the lacy outfit of the night before, but still just as alluring. Whatever Nick wore, he wore it well, whether it was a tailored suit or something a lot skimpier and slightly more unique.

Nick stopped by the edge of the table, his face impassively blank. "Ask me what?"

Theo waved a fork in the women's direction. "They were asking about you and Bailey, whether the two of you were dating. I am officially passing the buck and letting you answer that one."

There were two seats free at the table, one was right next to Cain, and the other at the complete opposite end. From Nick's current position, the one next to Cain was closest by far. Therefore, it stood to reason that he'd sit there. Cain braced himself, determined not to give anything away. They needed to talk first and quantify what the previous night had meant to them both, and where they wanted to go from there. And with Nick not having so much as glanced in Cain's direction, it wasn't as if he was getting any clues. In fact, going by the way Nick's gaze was firmly fixed on his brother, Cain was starting to get the impression that he was deliberately not letting his gaze stray in Cain's direction.

Carol had grown impatient waiting for Nick to answer Theo's question. "Come on, spill the details, my dear cousin. What's going on? Bailey's cute as fuck, so no one's exactly going to blame you for playing hide the sausage with him. Plus, he's absolutely loaded. You're always getting photographed together, so you're not really going to try and tell us there's absolutely nothing going on, are you? I bet at the very least, the two of you are friends with benefits?"

Cain's heart sank as Nick took the longer route toward the other end of the table. What the fuck was that? Was that a deliberate snub? Or was Nick just worried that they'd act suspiciously? Nick's gaze skated briefly over Cain as he eased himself into the seat next to an old friend of Rory's who'd been his best man. But it was so brief that it may as well not have existed—like Cain wasn't even there, or like Nick was trying to pretend that he wasn't.

Forgetting discretion altogether, Cain stared at Nick, willing him to meet his gaze in the hope that he'd at least get a brief smile, or some sort of recognition that Cain was alive and sat right in front of him. But Nick seemed oblivious as he helped himself to one of the pastries in the middle of the table before finally responding to Carol's question. "Bailey's just a friend.

Nothing more. He's not my type and I'm not his. Not really." Carol looked disappointed and, thankfully, the subject was dropped.

The rest of the breakfast proved torturous. No matter how many times Cain tried to catch Nick's eye, he may as well have been invisible. It was official. Nick was deliberately ignoring him. What did that mean? That he regretted last night? That it had just been a drunken mistake? That Theo almost discovering what they'd done had freaked him out? There were so many questions competing for space in Cain's brain that he felt dizzy with them. He wanted to stand up and ask them in front of everyone, demand to know what was going on. But of course he didn't; he stayed silent.

The longer the breakfast went on, the more miserable he became. To make it worse, Nick seemed fine: laughing and joking just as much as everyone else at the table. Had Cain let himself be used? Evidence would seem to suggest that that was the case. It hadn't felt like it last night, though. Nick had been just as into it as he'd been. He was sure of it. So why was he acting like this now?

"You alright?"

"Huh!?" Cain turned his head to find Theo staring at him, his brow creased with concern. He wondered how long his friend had been watching him. "I'm fine. Why?"

Theo's brows rose and he inclined his head toward the plate of food Cain had barely touched. "Cause you've barely eaten and you seem to have taken a vow of silence. I just wanted to check you hadn't dropped dead halfway through breakfast."

Cain forced a smile, even though it was the last thing he felt like doing. "Still breathing." Theo was still staring expectantly at him, so he felt he had to add more. "Just thinking about the drive back to London and all the stuff I need to do when I get home, that's all."

"Stuff?" Theo waggled his eyebrows suggestively. "Is this some of the secret stuff?"

Cain had almost forgotten, given everything else that had happened, that Theo knew his secret. He shook his head. "Nope. Nothing to do with that. I don't have anything booked until the week after next." That was the truth, he didn't. Not until a scheduled scene with Logan. Logan was cute and fun, and the thought of filming with him tasted like sawdust in his mouth after the night he'd spent with Nick. Nick had even managed to ruin that.

Seemingly oblivious to Cain's tension, Theo kept right on talking. "You should have traveled with me and Nick. I get to have a nap in the back of the car and leave all the driving to him."

Yeah, wouldn't that have been fun. Although, a tiny, malicious part of Cain's brain wondered how Nick would have managed to keep on ignoring him in the small confines of a car. He shrugged. "Yeah, well, I didn't. So, I'm driving back... on my own."

Theo stuck his lower lip out in an exaggerated pout, bringing a smile to Cain's face in spite of how shit he was feeling. He reached out a finger, pushing the protruding lip back to where it should be, Theo letting him before pretending to bite his finger. Theo relaxed back in his chair and sighed. "How long's your *stuff* going to take to do?" He wiggled his fingers in the air. "Can you come around tonight for a gaming marathon? Don't get me wrong. This wedding's been fun, but I've gone two whole days without playing and my fingers are getting twitchy."

Cain was torn. The distraction would be good. Far better than sitting at home and crying over Nick, but how much of a distraction was hanging out with Nick's brother really going to be? The two of them even had similar mannerisms. Add in that Theo would probably keep bringing his brother up in conversation and it sounded like hell. But then, Theo had been his friend way before he'd ever had feelings about Nick. Was he going to let him ruin that along with everything else? So he offered Theo a nod, his friend breaking out in a huge smile.

Cain lifted his head to look across the table, automatically seeking out the man who'd caused all the trouble. But with the breakfast party starting to say their farewells, the seat was empty. The fucking bastard had left without a word. If that didn't confirm that he'd been nothing more than a mistake, he didn't know what would.

Chapter Twelve

NICK

"So, you just ignored him? You fucked him and then ignored him?"

Nick lifted his head, from where he'd had it buried in his arms as he sprawled across Bailey's kitchen table, to meet his steady stare. "You're making it sound worse than it was." Bailey crossed his arms over his chest and continued to stare at Nick. When he'd turned up at his door without calling first, he hadn't been sure what he'd find. Anything was possible with Bailey. Thankfully, he'd been alone. Dressed up as if he was about to go out on a date, but alone. There was definitely nothing casual about the crimson off-the-shoulder jumper he wore, or the black jeans that may as well have been spray-painted on. And that was before you got to the perfectly styled blond hair and lip gloss. Nick checked his watch; it was three in the afternoon. After the drive back to London, he'd sought out Bailey before even going home. "Were you just on your way out? It's a bit early, isn't it?"

The stare turned decidedly frosty. "Don't change the subject. We're talking about you, not me."

"I wasn't changing the subject. I just didn't want to be taking up your valuable time if there's somewhere else you need to be."

Bailey leaned his hip against the sink, his head cocking to one side. "Oh, so you're going for the poor Nick angle, are you?"

"No!" Nick cringed at the defensive tone in his voice. "I just needed some advice and I *thought* you might be able to offer some. But you just seem pissed off at me."

The laugh that escaped Bailey's mouth didn't exactly exude sympathy either. He arched an eyebrow. "Do you know who I wish had come here for advice?" Sensing it was a rhetorical question, Nick didn't bother to try and provide an answer. He was proved right when Bailey kept on talking. "Cain. I wish he'd come to me for advice because do you know what I would have told him?" Nick gritted his teeth and kept silent as Bailey twisted the knife. "I would have told him to run away as fast as he could, that you weren't worth the effort."

"That's a bit mean."

Bailey levered himself away from the sink and stalked toward him before dropping into the seat opposite, his expression intense. "Let's look at the evidence, shall we? He tells you that he's had a thing for you for years and tries to kiss you. You say thanks, but no, thanks—"

"I didn't... I..." Nick fell silent again at the warning glance he ended up on the receiving end of. Bailey could be a teddy bear when he wanted, but he could also be a ferocious panther when he felt it was warranted. And it didn't take a genius to work out his current frame of mind.

Bailey continued as if he'd never been interrupted in the first place. "And then you run away. Things get heated between the two of you on the dance floor, and what do you do? You run away again."

"I didn't run. My family was there. Theo was there. I just removed myself from the situation for both of our sakes."

"Then"—Bailey held up a finger to punctuate his point—"he appears in your hotel room." He paused for a moment, his brow wrinkling. "How did he get in? You said you were in the bathroom."

Nick shrugged. The thought had crossed his mind. Not at the time, strangely. He'd been more concerned about other things. But later, there'd been only one possible conclusion. "My brother and I always get a spare keycard for each other's rooms. He must have convinced Theo to hand it over."

"Huh! Well, however he got in..." Bailey's lips twitched with the first glimmer of humor Nick had seen from him since he'd arrived and spilled all the details. He waved a hand up and down Nick's body. "...he saw you in all your splendor and liked it." He paused for a moment, his smile growing wider. "Lace or silk?"

Nick glared at him. "What?"

Bailey continued to smile at him, unabashed. "Just trying to get a visual picture with *all* the facts on which to base my advice."

"Oh, so you are going to offer some? I was beginning to think you were just going to have a go at me."

Bailey leaned forward, his chin resting on his hand. "One thing at a time." And then he just stared at Nick.

Nick caved relatively quickly, hoping the venom in his eyes said that he'd answer the question, but that he didn't like doing it. "Lace."

"What color?"

"Hardly relevant."

"Humor me."

"Blue."

"Pale blue or a darker blue, like..." Bailey scanned the kitchen, his gaze finally settling on a pair of oven gloves. "...them?"

Nick sighed. He should have just gone straight home. "Darker. Like a royal blue."

Bailey nodded. "Nice."

The reminder was making parts of Nick twitch that he really didn't want to be twitching while he was sat in Bailey's kitchen. It was also serving as a reminder of just how hot last night had been, how incredible it had been to find someone who not only didn't mind him wearing the panties but had asked him to leave them on while he fucked him. Bailey was right about him being a dick, but as he'd already explained to him, his actions that morning had been fueled by two things: Cain not being there when he'd woken up, and the panic that they hadn't discussed Nick's secret being a, well, secret. "What if he does tell someone?"

Bailey's eye roll said that he was a lost cause. "Why would he? And who's he going to tell?"

"Theo, maybe."

Bailey shook his head. "Can you imagine that conversation? Hey, guess what. Your brother gets off on wearing women's underwear. But it's okay because I find it incredibly hot and I got him to keep them on while he fucked me."

When Bailey put it like that, Nick couldn't imagine it. Not at all. But he hadn't been thinking clearly that morning, or since, apparently. He hadn't turned up at the wedding breakfast with the intention of ignoring Cain, even after waking up alone. But once he'd gotten there, he just wasn't sure that he could look in his direction without going beetroot red. And it wasn't like Carol—she, who saw everything—would have missed it. She would have been on him in a flash. So it had seemed safer to avoid looking Cain's way, and then once he'd started it had just been easier to continue in the same vein.

For all he knew, Cain hadn't been bothered. Except deep down he knew he would have been, that Nick had hurt him. Again. But then why had Cain left without speaking to him that morning? He felt like he was missing something. He ran his fingers through his hair as he tried to get some perspective on the whole thing. The past was the past; he couldn't do anything about it. All he could affect was the future. But he didn't know where to start.

Bailey broke into his thoughts. "And even if Cain was the type to kiss and tell, which hell, he might be, I don't know him. But if he was, you could just as easily spread it around that he makes porn. The way I see it, you're both in possession of a secret about the other."

Nick bristled at the intimation. "I wouldn't do that. I didn't even tell my own brother."

Bailey shrugged. "Well, there you go, then. So... let's get to the crux of the matter. What are you going to do now?"

Nick sighed. "That was where I was hoping you were going to come in."

A look of contemplation settled on Bailey's face. "Do you like him? And don't give me a load of bollocks about liking him because you've known him for years and he's your brother's friend. You know what I'm asking. You already know he's into you, so the ball's firmly in your court. You may have been an absolutely reprehensible human being toward him but you *might* be able to claw it back if that's what you want."

"How?"

Bailey stared at him incredulously. "Oh my God, remind me if I ever get in trouble with the law to get someone else to represent me, would you? Someone who is capable of thinking with more than one brain cell." He huffed out a sigh. "Talking to him would be a good start. You know, the bit you didn't bother to do this morning."

"He left before I woke up. Maybe he was already avoiding me before I started avoiding him." Nick cringed as soon as the sentence left his mouth, aware that he sounded like a sulky teenager. He sat up straight, filling his lungs with air and reminding himself that he was closer to thirty than he was to twenty. "You're right. I'll go and see him. I'll apologize for this morning. I'll ask him why he crept out without waking me instead of jumping to conclusions, and I'll tell him..."

"You'll tell him, what?"

"I'll tell him that the gift he gave me last night was something wonderful, and that I'm incredibly attracted to him, and that I think there could be something more than just sex between us. I'll..."

Bailey rolled his eyes. "Yeah, yeah. I don't need to hear the whole speech. You're telling the wrong person. Now, piss off. I've got better things to do than listen to you whine all day about the things you keep doing to make life difficult for yourself."

Nick stood, leaning his weight on the back of the chair he'd just been sitting on. "Things or a person?" The quirk of Bailey's lips was enough for Nick to know the answer without confirmation. It was strange though. It wasn't like Bailey to be keeping secrets. He was usually the first to regale Nick with what he'd been up to, whether he wanted to hear it or not. Nick needed to dig a bit deeper to find out what was going on there. But not today. He needed to sort out his own shit today. The shit he'd created.

NICK FROZE, HIS KNUCKLES almost—but not quite—touching the door. What reception was he going to get? Not good, that was for sure. But there were different degrees of not good, from Cain glowering at him to slamming the door in his face. Glowering he could take. At least that would mean Cain was prepared to listen to him. Cain slamming the door in his face, however, would provide a logistical nightmare.

Before he could overthink himself into complete immobility, he knocked. Cain might not even be in. During the drive back, Theo had said that Cain was coming straight back to London, but his brother didn't know absolutely everything. His ignorance at Cain's porn career proved that.

There was the sound of footsteps approaching the door and then it swung open to reveal Cain framed in the doorway. *Definitely in, then.* Cain's face gave nothing away as he crossed his arms over his chest and stared at Nick without saying a word.

Nick almost found himself wishing for the door slam. At least then Cain would have been exhibiting some emotion. Whereas this impassive facade just said that Cain was done. Done with Nick, and all the crap that came along with him, which meant that this had been a wasted journey. It was hard to work out what to say when all his pre-rehearsed speeches on the way over had centered on Cain being angry at him.

Nick was silent for so long, words and emotions tumbling through his brain, that Cain stepped back, the door starting to close. At least that geared Nick into action. He lunged forward, shoving his body into the shrinking gap. "Wait! I know you're annoyed at me and you have every right to be, given the fact that I behaved abominably this morning. I should never have ignored you. It was childish and an absolute dick move that probably made you feel like shit, and made it seem like last night meant absolutely nothing to me, which isn't true... but I was scared that you might tell someone about me... about my secret. Which I should have known you wouldn't if I'd been thinking clearly. But I wasn't, obviously. Or I wouldn't be here now groveling and hoping that you'll listen to me. But when you were gone when I woke up, my mind started playing tricks on me."

Nick had said some of the things he'd planned to, but nowhere in his pre-visit plan had he planned to spill them all in the space of about three seconds with all the aplomb of a toddler that had just learned to speak. It was no wonder confusion had replaced the blank expression. Nick wasn't sure if that was better or worse. He made an attempt to gather a bit of poise from somewhere, trying to channel the Nick who regularly ruled the roost in the courtroom. "We need to talk. Can I come in so we can talk, please?"

Cain gave a brief nod before letting go of the door and sauntering into his living room. Nick closed the door and followed him, finding him standing by the window, his gaze fixed on something outside. Either that or it was just an excuse so he didn't have to look at Nick. Nick let his gaze run all over the other man while his attention was elsewhere. God, he was gorgeous. It hit him again how blind he'd been not to notice it. They might not have run into each other that often over the last couple of years, but he had seen him. He just hadn't *seen* him. Well, his eyes were definitely open now.

"I thought you wanted to talk?"

They were the first words Cain had spoken since Nick's arrival, and enough to snap him out of his reverie. He seated himself on the sofa, figuring he'd be waiting for a very long time if he waited for an invitation. "I do. Just trying to work out where to start."

"Maybe start by explaining more about why you acted like a dick this morning.

You keep telling me you're sorry, but then you pull yet another stunt."

"I am sorry. Really, I am. For my behavior at the party, how I treated you on the dance floor, *and* for this morning."

Cain turned to face him, his face shadowed. "The rest I could take. But this morning"—he shook his head—"that really hurt. It made me feel like I'd just been used. We had sex last night, Nick, and then this morning I might as well have been a stranger to you. Were you drunk last night? Theo said he thought you were drunk. Did you only sleep with me because I happened to be available and you weren't thinking straight?"

"God, no!" Nick stood without conscious thought, closing the space between them until he stood directly in front of Cain. "I was a bit tipsy at the wedding but I'd already sobered up by the time you turned up in my room." He paused, the unanswered mystery coming to mind. "How did you get in anyway? Did you take Theo's keycard?"

Cain nodded. "Yeah, sorry about that." His lips quivered into a semi-smile. "I can see now that me turning up must have been one hell of a surprise to you."

Nick snorted. "Yeah, it was. I never..." He hesitated, unsure whether he was ready to be that honest. But then if nothing else, Cain had earned that. He took a deep breath and just let the words come. "I never thought I'd ever meet someone who looked at me with that much desire when I was wearing, well, you know, you saw. You made me feel like I wasn't a freak."

"You're not a freak." Cain's brow furrowed. "Is that what you think?"

Nick shrugged, attempting to hide the memories that still had the power to hurt him under a layer of affected casualness. "I've been told before that I was."

"By who?"

Cain taking offense on his behalf was beyond sweet. It made a warm glow spread through Nick's body. "By past boyfriends."

"Wankers!"

"And that's only the ones I told. The rest, I didn't even dare mention it to them. Some of them would have been absolutely horrified if they'd ever found out." Nick paused, taking a moment to consider that being this honest actually felt good. "You should have been more shocked. Why weren't you?" The words sounded almost like an accusation.

Cain grinned. "I kind of had other things on my mind, like how fucking hot you looked. I didn't know that's something

I could ever be into. But on you..." He looked sheepish, twin spots of color appearing on his cheeks.

"So, you really liked it?" Nick knew he was being needy, knew he was seeking validation, but he just couldn't stop himself.

"Yeah." Cain's voice was husky. "I really liked it. Will you tell me about it?"

This was the point at which Nick usually changed the subject. Even with Bailey, it was still something he avoided discussing, no matter how much Bailey insisted on bringing it up at every opportunity. He didn't do it maliciously, but because he honestly seemed to believe that the first step to acceptance was talking about it. But this was Cain. The man he'd stood completely exposed in front of, literally and figuratively, and all he'd gotten was desire and encouragement. No judgement. No scorn. Just the acceptance that he couldn't seem to give himself. Nick started to pace, needing movement in order to be able to get the words out. "I think it started when I was about thirteen. I knew I liked looking at pictures of women in their underwear but I figured that was normal. All part of puberty. Then I started to notice boys, so I thought I was bisexual. It took me about another year to realize that the girls themselves did absolutely nothing for me, just their underwear." He risked a glance in Cain's direction but the only expression on his face was curiosity. "But like I said, most people don't get it." He gave a wry smile. "Not sure I get it myself to be honest. I've tried to stop, but I never last very long."

"Is it just lace?"

Nick shook his head. "No. It depends what mood I'm in. I like silk as well." It felt strangely cleansing to be able to be so blunt about it, and still there was no judgment.

In fact, the gleam from the night before was back in Cain's eyes. "I'd like to see that." He seemed to catch himself as if remembering that he was meant to hate Nick's guts rather than be propositioning him. He turned back to the window, continuing his earlier scrutiny of whatever he'd deemed so fascinating.

It felt like the brick wall between them was firmly back in place, and all Nick wanted to do was take a sledgehammer and smash it down. He perched on the arm of the sofa. "Why did you sneak out without waking me this morning?"

Cain spun around, his eyes wide. "I didn't sneak out. Theo called to say he was on his way to my room. We were about five minutes away from him knowing what we'd been up to." His chin jutted out as he walked over to Nick, looking down at him. "But I told you that this morning before I left."

It was Nick's turn to be confused. He searched through his recollections of that morning but there was nothing prior to waking up and finding the room empty. "Did I answer you?"

Cain blinked. "Well, no, but you made a few noises. I thought you were awake." Comprehension slowly dawned on his face. "You weren't awake. You thought I'd just left?"

Nick nodded. "Yeah, I woke up and you weren't there. It made it feel like..." He thought about it carefully, wanting to be honest without being dramatic. "...like you might have regretted it and couldn't wait to get out of there."

The strangled laugh that escaped Cain's throat held very little humor. "Are you serious? A couple of weeks ago I told you I'd had a thing for you since I was fourteen. How do you get from that to me regretting it? That's a huge leap to make, even for you." He paused, grimacing. "Oh, I get it. You're so hung up on the fact that you think you're a freak that you just can't imagine that anyone could know the truth about you and still want you. Is that it?"

He'd pretty much hit the nail on the head. Nick managed a strangled "yes" around the sudden lump in his throat. While he hadn't exactly expected sympathy from Cain, he would have hoped for more than the eye roll he got in response. First Bailey, now Cain. Nick had never felt more pathetic. He dropped his gaze to study the carpet, only raising it again when Cain nudged Nick's thigh with his knee.

Cain sighed. "I'm sorry you thought I'd run out on you, but you really should have known better. I've given you no reason to doubt that anything I've said has been anything but the truth. Would you rather Theo had discovered us together?"

Nick shook his head, feeling like a prize idiot. Cain was right. He should have known better, should have trusted him enough to know that he wouldn't have done that. He'd always slept like the dead. It had even been a running joke between him and a previous boyfriend. So he had no doubt that Cain was telling the truth when he said he'd tried to wake him, or thought he had managed to. It was a shame the same clarity had been missing that morning.

All he'd had to do was act like a normal person over breakfast and then corner Cain to talk to him afterwards. It seemed like ever since Cain's revelation at the party, he'd been making an absolute hash of everything. Actually, maybe it was before that: the point at which he'd realized who it was he'd been lusting after. "I'm sorry. I seem to make really bad decisions when it comes to you. You mess with my head."

The way Cain tilted his head to one side and scrutinized Nick made it clear he wasn't quite sure how to take that statement. Had Nick put his foot in it again? Cain finally put his question into words. "In a good way, or...?"

Nick acted completely on impulse, reaching out to grab Cain's hand in order to interlock their fingers together, a feeling of weightlessness descending upon him when Cain didn't try and pull away. "Yeah, in a good way." Cain stared down at their joined hands, his skin, with that year-round Mediterranean tan, a lot darker than Nick's. However, his face didn't give a lot away, so Nick couldn't work out what he was thinking.

Cain finally tore his gaze away from their hands. "Did you just come around to apologize, or were you after something else?"

He hadn't really thought past the apology part. It had seemed like way too much of a stretch given the morning's events to assume he'd get past the apology. Only, Nick was holding Cain's hand, right? And he'd initiated that. Not Cain. And weirdly, it felt a lot more intimate than anything they'd done the previous night. Then there was the glimmer of hope lurking in Cain's stare to consider. If Cain could forgive that quickly, then Nick needed to be oh so careful. He had to be sure that it was what he really wanted before he messed around with him any more than he had already. Cain might have turned into someone incredibly hot—almost overnight in Nick's eyes—but he was also a friend, someone he cared about. He went for honesty, seeing as it had served him pretty well up to this point. "I don't know. I hadn't thought that far ahead. I figured I might need a hospital once you were done with me."

Cain smiled, moving forward so that his thighs slotted in between Nick's, pushing them wider apart. "I'm a great believer in making love, not war."

Awareness prickled along Nick's skin, every part of his body incredibly sensitized where it touched Cain's. It was obvious that this thing between them—whatever it was—wasn't over. Not by a long shot. He swallowed, trying to bring some much-needed saliva to a mouth that was suddenly bereft of it. He'd given up any chance of fighting his attraction when he'd slept with Cain the night before. Trying to resist it now was a bit like closing the stable door after the horse had already bolted. He slid the hand that wasn't still entwined with Cain's up his thigh, feeling the muscles contract through the denim as he peered up at the younger man from beneath his eyelashes. "I'm not a fan of war myself, and I think we've already created enough stress for ourselves for one day. So maybe the first one is the better option."

A slow smile spread across Cain's face. "I was hoping you'd say that." He curled a hand around Nick's neck, his thumb lightly brushing Nick's earlobe in a caress that really shouldn't have felt so damn good considering it was only his ear. "We should go back to your place."

Nick caught hold of Cain's hand, stilling it in order to allow him to think for a few seconds. "What's wrong with here?"

Cain winked. "I don't have what you like here."

Oh! Nick struggled for a response. "I don't have to... I can..." He didn't want Cain thinking he was someone who couldn't even get it up without the stimulation of women's underwear, or they were right back in freak territory.

Cain's brow furrowed. "You prefer it though, right? It makes it better?"

Nick nodded. "Yeah, but..." For fuck's sake, it would help if he could manage to finish a sentence. "I just..." He shook his head in frustration when words still wouldn't come out. "I don't want you thinking that you have to..."

The thumb had started moving again, this time sweeping down to caress Nick's jaw. "Would it help if I said I wanted to see? That I'd suggested it more for me, than for you? It turns me on, Nick. I thought I'd succeeded in showing you that last night. It's a part of you. A part that I find incredibly intriguing... and hot. Will you let me? Please."

There was no way of arguing with an impassioned plea like that, or with the look of longing in Cain's eyes. All Nick could do was nod. What the hell had last night started? He felt like a pebble rolling downhill, gradually gathering more and more speed and unable to stop.

Chapter Thirteen

CAIN

Never had one day felt more like a roller coaster. After the euphoria of waking up with Nick and recalling the previous night, suffering through the wedding breakfast had seemed like the cruelest kind of purgatory. Cain had ridden that wave of emotion the whole journey back, trying to remind himself that he hadn't lost anything—not really. You couldn't lose what you'd never had in the first place. He refused to be made to feel dirty and used when he'd done nothing wrong. How he was ever going to be able to look Nick in the face again was another matter entirely.

He'd figured he'd have a few weeks before having to face that obstacle. Theo's upcoming birthday to be more precise. And then, lo and behold, Nick had turned up at his door, full of apologies and begging for a chance to explain. It had been difficult to hold a grudge once he'd discovered why Nick had acted the way he had. Nick believing he'd snuck out without a word put a whole different complexion on what had happened between them. If only Cain had waited long enough to be sure that Nick was awake, or failing that, he could have sent a text. He was definitely at least partly to blame for the morning's fiasco.

Besides, this was Nick. The man he'd adored in spite of his failings for the last ten years, so it was doubtful he could have summoned the willpower to send him away, no matter what Cain thought he'd done. It was obvious that underneath Nick's impenetrable exterior that he showed to the world, he was actually quite vulnerable. He'd guarded his secret so zealously that it clouded his judgment. Not that his idiot ex-boyfriends had helped matters either. Even talking about his fetish made Nick beautifully flustered.

Just as he was now that they were standing in Nick's bedroom.

Cheeks flaming, Nick lifted a hand, waving vaguely in the direction of the chest of drawers at the far side of the room. "In there."

Barely able to keep the smirk off his face at Nick's obvious discomfort, Cain walked across the room, pausing to look back over his shoulder when Nick didn't follow. He looked like he'd become frozen to the spot, his eyes downcast. "Which drawer?"

"The bottom one." Nick's voice sounded like he'd been gargling with razorblades. Cain felt slightly guilty for finding his awkwardness adorable. But then, Nick had given him enough shit over the past few weeks that he deserved to get a bit back. Besides, this was for Nick's own good. A way of showing him that his sexual predilections weren't the crime of the century and that there were men in the world—like Cain—that were perfectly fine with it. "I was hoping that you were going to show me, but I guess since you're still all the way over there that I'll just take a look myself. Is that alright?"

When the only response was a strangled noise that could have meant anything, Cain went ahead and eased the drawer open anyway. Pulling the towel away that lay over the top, Cain stared down at the drawer's contents, letting out a long, low whistle. He hadn't given much thought to what he might see, maybe about half a dozen pairs. But this was a far cry from that: the whole drawer packed full of myriad fabrics and colors.

Was that why Nick had been so worried? He guessed that every secret had layers. There was the top layer and then there were the underlying layers when you dug even deeper. And this was definitely digging deeper. The collection he was staring at had to have been collated over a number of years.

He crouched down, letting his gaze run slowly over everything he could see, his imagination already running riot. He'd already seen Nick in lace. He wanted to see him in something else. A flash of scarlet caught his eye from the corner of the drawer where it was almost hidden. He stuck his hand in, grabbing the piece of material and holding it up to get a better look. It was a silky G-string consisting of very little material. Cain stood, turning back to face Nick, his cock already starting to push against the zipper of his trousers in anticipation.

He held the panties up so that Nick could see them. "Would you wear these for me?" If he'd thought that Nick's cheeks had been red before, that was nothing in comparison to how they were now. They were so red, they almost matched the underwear in question. Nick's tongue darted out to moisten his lips, which did absolutely nothing to help Cain's state of arousal. Was he pushing him too fast? It was less than twenty-four hours since Cain had inadvertently walked in on Nick in the hotel bathroom. It wasn't as if Nick had shared his secret willingly. Cain had barged his way into it. And now he'd barged into his house and bedroom as well.

He lowered his hand, feeling like the worst sort of idiot. The last thing he wanted to do while trying to make things better was make them worse. "I'm sorry. It wasn't my intention to make you feel uncomfortable. I can be a bit too pushy sometimes."

At least the apology seemed to break through the frozen veneer that had held Nick in its thrall ever since they'd set foot in the bedroom. He closed the space between the two of them, the ghost of a smile hovering on his lips. "You were always pushy, even as a kid. Remember that day when I only had two tickets for the car show and you demanded that you got to go as well as Theo. You went and sat in the back of the car and refused to move, no matter how long my dad tried to reason with you. We ended up having to ring around and find another ticket for you."

Cain did remember. He also remembered the real reason he'd been so adamant that he got to go, and it had absolutely nothing to do with a love of cars and everything to do with Nick. Given that the secret was well and truly out, there didn't seem to be any point in not being truthful. "I just wanted to spend the day with you. I was jealous that Theo got to have you all to himself. I don't even like cars."

Nick smiled. "I know. You barely left my side that day. It was like I'd grown a new shadow. I couldn't work out why you found me so fascinating. I was just a skinny teenager."

"A skinny but hot teenager."

"If you say so." Nick wrapped his hand around Cain's wrist, lifting it until the red silk hung between them, both their gazes fastened on it. "You realize you've probably picked out the skimpiest pair I have?"

Cain shrugged. He didn't care about skimpy. He just wanted to see the red against Nick's skin and, if he was honest, he was just as enthusiastic about seeing what Nick's ass would look like in the G-string. "They were the ones that caught my attention."

"Who do you want me to wear them for? Me or you?"

Cain gave the question a due amount of consideration. "Me." Nick's eyes widened at Cain's revelation. He obviously hadn't believed what Cain had told him earlier. Cain felt the need to offer more of an explanation. "I don't think it's so much the underwear, as *you* in the underwear. Knowing it turns you on, turns me on as well. Does that make sense?"

"I guess so." Nick pulled them out of his hand. "Ask me again."

Cain adopted the most seductive voice he could manage, pulling on all his EagerBoyz knowledge and experience of what drove the subscribers wild. "Could you please put these on for me? I'm desperate to see what they look like on you." He took Nick's hand and pressed it to his crotch, Nick's fingers curling around his erection for a few seconds before falling away. If that wasn't proof that he was telling the truth, then nothing was.

Nick's nod was jerky and disjointed, his breathing ragged. His gaze swept toward the bathroom. "Where? Here, or do you want a big reveal?"

"Here." Cain changed his mind as soon as the word had left his mouth. "No! Scrap that. I don't want to see you until you're wearing them." He was aware that he was being pushy again, but then Nick had put him firmly in the driver's seat, so what did he expect. He made himself comfortable on a chair to wait as Nick disappeared out of sight into the bathroom. After a few minutes, he started to worry. How long could it possibly take to shed your clothes and don a tiny piece of fabric? "Nick?"

"Yeah?" The voice was muffled.

"Just checking you're still there. I thought you might have escaped out of the window or something."

"I live on the fourth floor. And this is not the outfit I want to be rushed to hospital in. I can assure you of that."

Cain chuckled to himself, imagining the ensuing scandal. "So what's taking so long?"

"It's not really working."

He frowned, trying to work out what Nick could possibly mean. "What isn't?"

A weary sigh echoed from the bathroom. "They're quite small. My cock... well, isn't at the moment."

"Oh, right." The mental image of Nick struggling to contain his erection within the small scrap of fabric made Cain's ass hole clench. "I don't mind." *Understatement of the day.*

And then Nick appeared in the doorway, Cain forcing himself to keep his eyes on his face for long torturous seconds, taking in the mussed blond hair and the flushed cheeks. He slowly let his gaze drift down Nick's torso, past the slight tufts of blond hair he had around his nipples that were so fair you could hardly see them, along his treasure trail, and finally to where the red silk clung to him. He'd done his best to cover his cock, but to say it was straining for release wouldn't do it justice, the material already damp with Nick's arousal.

Nick made a noise in his throat. "Sorry. As soon as I feel the silk against my skin, it gets me going."

"You don't need to apologize." Cain was dizzy with want. He thought he'd been horny the night before, but that was nothing compared to how he felt now. He wanted Nick to throw him down on the carpet, push straight into him and pound his ass. No, not wanted. Needed. He needed everything Nick had to give and more.

He forced himself to breathe, trying to temper the desire that sped through his veins to something more manageable, something he could control. "Turn around." Nick offered a slightly sheepish smile before obliging. Cain found himself staring at a muscular ass bisected by the tiny strip of material. His breath escaped in a whoosh, his body flooding with heat. "So fucking hot."

And then there was no more worrying about playing it cool. There was just the burning need to get naked, his hands fumbling at his clothes as he ripped them off piece by piece. Once he was naked, Nick could fuck him, and he could get some respite from the alien which had taken over his body and made him feel like a different person. He made porn, for Christ's sake. He was meant to be good at making it last for hours. It was part of his job. But one glance at Nick in sexy underwear, and it was like the fourteen-year-old who'd weaved numerous fantasies about Nick was back with a vengeance. As if he'd been waiting for this opportunity before being able to grow up.

Cain barely had three seconds to appreciate his lack of clothes before Nick's lips slammed down on his. He was all roving hands, tongue, and teeth, and Cain loved it. It was precisely what he needed. If last night had been a gentle introduction, then this was the both of them letting go. He had no idea which of them initiated the tumble to the floor, only that he found himself on his back on the carpet, his hips grinding in a rhythm that pushed his stiff cock against Nick's silk-covered one. He buried his fingers in Nick's hair, refusing to let go of his mouth as he drowned in his taste.

When a lube-covered finger probed at his ass, Cain gratefully lifted his leg, wrapping his thigh around Nick's hip to give him more room. The whine he let out as Nick's finger slid deep sounded nothing like Cain. It was like some sort of demon had taken over his body and wouldn't be satisfied until it had taken everything Nick had to offer. When Nick's finger rubbed over Cain's prostate, Cain almost came there and then. He tore his mouth away from Nick's, grabbing hold of his wrist and stilling it. "Steady."

Nick grinned at him, self-satisfaction bordering on smugness exuding from him in spades. "Sensitive, aren't you?" He made an attempt to overcome Cain's tight grip but Cain had already foreseen such an eventuality and held firm, his fingers a vice around Nick's wrist.

"No, you don't."

Nick's gaze drifted over Cain's body in a heated caress which was almost as good as being touched. "When did you get to be so hot?"

"A while ago, you just didn't notice. You were too busy calling me squirt and seeing me as nothing more than an extension of Theo." Cain shifted, regretting it when the finger that was still embedded inside him brushed over the exact spot he'd been trying so hard to prevent it from touching, sparks of sensation shooting down his spine. "Jesus! You need to fuck me. Before I come."

Nick eased his finger loose and patted Cain's ass. "I can do that. Turn over."

Cain did, burying his face in the carpet and spreading his thighs as Nick moved to straddle him, his silk-encased balls brushing Cain's skin and raising goosebumps. He lay still as Nick carried out a thorough exploration, his fingers tracing the muscles of Cain's back before giving the arms folded beneath Cain's head the same attention. Then those same hands moved to Cain's ass, pulling his cheeks apart. Once upon a time Cain might have felt self-conscious, but that ship had sailed a long time ago, ever since he'd realized just how close the camera got when he was filming porn scenes. It was hard to get hung up when millions of people had viewed the exact same sight Nick was taking so long to scrutinize. "Does it meet with your—"

The rest of Cain's question was lost in a strangled gasp as the wet warmth of Nick's tongue started to become acquainted with the area. Cain arched up, pushing back in a movement intended to offer encouragement. "Fuck! You're going to kill me." There was no answer, not surprising really considering that Nick's tongue was busy fucking his hole, alternating between soft little licks and harder stabs of his tongue. Cain writhed beneath him, unable to work out which was worse. Or better. He couldn't even decide whether he wanted it to stop, or go on forever. "God, your tongue. I've heard about your tongue... in the courtroom... how good it is. But I had no idea it was this talented." Cain knew he was making very little sense, but it gave him something else to think about other than the overwhelming desire to come.

And then all of a sudden, the drugging torment stopped as Nick spoke. "I don't know what you've heard, but I can assure you that I've never done this in the courtroom."

Cain let his head hit the floor with a *thunk*, unable to keep a stupid grin off his face. "Are you sure? You've got a very impressive success rate. Are you sure you haven't slipped the judges a bit of tongue on occasion?" There was a crinkle of foil from behind him, Cain not needing to turn around to know what that signified. Relief rushed through him at the thought of finally getting to come.

"Quite sure. Have you seen the judges? Most of them are crusty old men. I'd rather lose every single case than put any of my appendages anywhere near them."

Cain forced himself to breathe slow and deep, trying to stave off the insistent ache in his balls. "How about you use one of those appendages on me?"

"Sure. Any preference? Arm? Leg? Maybe—"

"Give me your goddamn cock! Now's not the time to suddenly develop a sense of humor."

"Ouch! That's mean. I ought to keep you waiting a bit longer for that dig."

Thankfully, Nick's actions didn't match his words, and Cain forced himself to relax as the blunt intrusion of Nick's cock nudged at his entrance. But unfortunately, nudge was all it did. He let out an exasperated sigh. "I hate you, Nick." *I love you, Nick.* There was no way he was letting those words escape though. He'd only just gotten Nick to see him properly. It was way too soon to risk him running in the opposite direction. He'd like to think that a time would come when he could say them, but he was probably getting way ahead of himself.

Nick leaned forward, covering Cain's body with his own and pushing all other thoughts out of Cain's head as he finally gave him what he'd been begging for, for the last God knows how long. Cain spread his thighs wider as the delicious stretch intensified until Nick was fully seated inside him, and it was hard to work out where Nick started and he ended.

"Okay?"

Cain turned his head, meeting the concerned expression of his lover. Ha! Nick was his lover. Even crammed full of his cock, it was hard to wrap his head around that piece of information. Cain nodded, his hips already starting to move of their own accord, needing more than just the blissful sensation of being full. He smiled. "Yeah. More than okay." Nick mirrored his smile, dipping his head so that they could share a kiss and swallowing Cain's gasps as Nick began to thrust—long, deep thrusts that sent bursts of pure sensation spiraling through Cain's body. Sweat broke out on both of their bodies as they began to move together in earnest.

Despite hovering on the edge of coming, Cain made an attempt to catalogue every moment: the way Nick's skin felt against his own, the glide of the silk panties that Nick still wore against Cain's ass as he thrust into him, the ragged hot breaths in his ear as Nick gasped out his own pleasure, and the way Nick's fingers dug into Cain's skin leaving indelible marks that would no doubt show up as bruises the next day. They were all his to keep forever, no matter what happened after.

But then there was nothing but pleasure invading every cell of Cain's body and wrapping its tingling fingers around every nerve ending and synapse. Cain gritted his teeth, wanting to hold on to that edge of pleasure for a few more seconds. But Nick didn't play fair, sneaking his hand under Cain's body and fisting his cock in time with his thrusts. It only took a few strokes before Cain was coming, screaming his completion into the carpet.

He lay there boneless, his cheek pressed into the carpet as he listened to Nick's grunts. Since when had he found grunting sexy? But then, that was love for you. Nick could probably blow his nose and he'd find it sweet and adorable. With one particularly loud grunt, Nick buried himself deep in Cain's ass, his body shuddering as he came. A few more seconds and he was sprawled on top of Cain, his arms wrapping around Cain's chest and his lips finding his neck.

THEY LAY ON THE FLOOR for at least ten minutes before either of them managed to muster the energy to transfer to the bed, which was all of about three meters away.

Once ensconced, Cain lifted his arm, examining a carpet burn on his forearm. He couldn't bring himself to care though, not when it had been so much fun to get it. He just wished Nick wasn't so quiet. It made the doubt start to creep in again. It was a shame he didn't smoke. At least then he would have had something to do with his hands. Instead, he found himself transfixed by the sight of the discarded condom which had become lodged on the side of the wastepaper bin where Nick had thrown it during their transfer from floor to bed. Finally, Cain couldn't take it anymore. Call him needy, but now that the buzz of arousal had gone, he needed clarification of where they stood and this void of nothingness wasn't doing it for him. "So... what was this, a two-night stand?" Needing to see Nick's face when he answered, Cain forced himself to turn in his direction. It was gratifying when barely a second passed before Nick shook his head.

"I hope not."

Cain couldn't stop the corners of his mouth from twitching up into a smile. He rolled onto his side so that he could prop himself up on one elbow, his smile growing wider as Nick's gaze immediately homed in on where Cain's muscles bunched. All of those hours spent in the gym suddenly seemed far more worthwhile. He gave Nick his best flirtatious look, his cock already beginning to stir in response to the expression on Nick's face. "Me too." The words probably weren't needed, but he said them anyway. There were still things, though, that he needed to get off his chest. One particular thing sprung to mind that still hadn't been resolved to his satisfaction and was like a thorn stuck under his skin. "What about Bailey?"

Nick laughed. He goddamn laughed.

Cain was halfway off the bed and in his head already halfway out the door when Nick grabbed his arm. He shook him off, bending over to pick up his trousers and stepping into them. "I'm glad you find it funny. Maybe you and him could have a good laugh about the poor sucker who's so hung up on you the next time you're in bed together. I'm guessing that you have some sort of open relationship, or... who the fuck knows. I don't care."

"You're jealous."

Cain paused from where he'd been trying to wrestle his arms into his shirt sleeves. "I just told you, I don't care." He was such a liar, and the worst thing was that it was plainly obvious.

Nick sat up in bed. "I didn't laugh because it was funny, I laughed because the idea is so ridiculous and I don't know why people are so convinced that we're a couple. They keep asking and asking, and no matter how many times I say no, they don't seem able to let it drop."

Cain forced himself to lift his head and look at Nick for the first time since his rapid departure from the bed. There was nothing but earnestness on his face. What the hell was he doing? They'd cleared up the misunderstanding from this morning, only for him to be so eager to create another one. He expected Nick to trust him, yet he wasn't willing to give him the same courtesy back. He'd never suffered from such crippling insecurity or irrationality before but Nick seemed to scramble his brains like no one else did—or could. At this rate, they weren't going to last two minutes.

He took a deep breath, forcing his fingers to uncurl from the death grip they still held on the shirt before seating himself gingerly on the edge of the bed. "Apparently you talk to him all the time. What am I supposed to think?"

"We're friends. Close friends. And yeah, in the interests of full disclosure, we slept together. Once. But it was years ago. Neither of us looks at the other one that way." Nick's voice softened. "And he's the only friend I've got that knows about..." He gestured in the direction of the bottom drawer which still lay open, just in case Cain was in any doubt what he was referring to. "He's been a great support the last few years. I owe him a lot. But there's nothing but friendship between the two of us. I'll swear on a bible if you want me to."

"I see." Cain really did see. He wasn't just saying that. Shared secrets had a habit of creating a bond like no other. He peered at Nick from beneath his lashes, feeling like the world's biggest idiot for overreacting. "Are you sure he's not got a thing for you?"

Nick's lips quirked. "Pretty damn sure, seeing as when I saw him earlier, he told me I was an absolute dick for the way I'd treated you and that he wished you were there so he could tell you to stay the hell away from me. Then he told me to come here and grovel. They were definitely not the actions of someone wanting to keep me all to himself."

Cain contemplated the new information that put Bailey in a completely different light. "I think I could come to like him."

Nick sprawled back against the pillows. "You probably will. He's a pain in the ass, but a likeable one at the same time." He patted the empty expanse of bed next to him. "Now that's sorted, why don't you come back to bed?"

It was incredibly tempting, but with adrenaline still coursing through his body, Cain wanted to get a few other things sorted first. If he did, it might mean that he could find a way to get over the insecurity that turned his brain to mush whenever he was around Nick. "It might be too soon to ask this question, but I'm going to do it anyway." He swallowed past the lump in his throat, the sudden attack of bravado already starting to desert him. "Me and you. What is it? A relationship, or just sex?" *Please don't say, just sex.* Cain was glad this time that Nick took longer to think about it. That way there was less chance of him saying something he didn't mean.

Nick sat up straight again. "I already know you. I mean not everything, but a lot of things. We're a long way from strangers. We've been part of each other's lives for years. So"—his brow wrinkled—"I don't see how it could just be sex. I wouldn't do that to you. For one, Theo would skin me alive."

Cain hid his smile by ducking his head and pretending a greater concentration than necessary to unbutton his trousers again. By the time he'd shucked them off and climbed back into the bed, he'd calmed himself down enough to just mutter a very understated "good." Any last vestiges of giddiness were wiped away by a very sobering thought coming to mind. "So, if it's a relationship... which one of us is going to tell Theo?"

The expression on Nick's face said that the idea was just as repugnant to him as it was to Cain. "Neither of us. Not yet, anyway."

Cain didn't like the thought of keeping secrets from him. Although, he supposed that was pretty hypocritical considering the amount of time he'd been making porn behind his best friend's back. Theo probably still wouldn't be any the wiser if it hadn't been for Nick stumbling across him at the party. Still, it didn't sit right with him. "The longer we leave it, the worse it will be. If he finds out we've been keeping things from him, he'll never forgive either of us."

Nick moved across the bed and crawled on top of Cain, his lips hovering a few inches away. "Let's not talk about Theo at the moment. I can think of more interesting things to do."

It was obvious that Nick was trying to distract him, but it was also no secret how weak Cain was when it came to Nick. There'd be plenty of time later to work out the best way to break the news to Theo. Right now, they should be celebrating the fact that they'd just agreed that they were in a relationship. Who'd have thought it—a relationship with Nick, the man he'd craved for years? It was hard to believe that the events of the past twenty-four hours weren't just a dream. Yeah, Nick was right. Any problems could wait a bit longer. Cain lifted his head, sealing their lips together and feeling Nick's cock starting to harden against his thigh.

Chapter Fourteen

NICK

Nick's eyes met Cain's in the mirror as he knotted his tie. Out of the last nine nights, he'd stayed over eight of them, And Nick would have been lying if he said he hadn't missed him on the one night he hadn't.

Once they'd agreed that what they were doing was a relationship, they seemed to have gone from zero to sixty in the same space of time it might have taken another couple to arrange a date. Getting closer had definitely been helped by the fact that Nick had already organized taking time off after the wedding. Apart from Cain's shifts at the restaurant, that had left them free to do all the things new couples usually did: dates, getting to know each other properly, and sex. There had definitely been lots of sex.

Today was Nick's first day back at work. He loved his job and he wasn't used to feeling like there was somewhere else he'd rather be. Another thing that was new were the butterflies that started up in his stomach whenever Cain looked at him the way he was doing right now, like he wanted to peel Nick's clothes off with his teeth and then lick him all over—which wouldn't be the first time.

They'd had sex with and without the underwear in the past week, Nick relieved to realize that it accentuated their sex life but wasn't the be all and end all. "You can't be looking at me that way when I'm on my way to work."

Cain appeared behind him in the mirror, wrapping his arms around his waist and resting his head on Nick's shoulder. "I can't help myself. It's the suit. You don't know how many dreams I've had about Nicholas Hackett finding me guilty of a crime and then punishing me in his own special way."

"I don't know if that's hot... or disturbing."

Cain's smile was full of mischief. "Let's go with hot." His hand slid under Nick's suit jacket, delving into the waistband of his trousers.

Nick slapped his hand away, not needing to ask what Cain was searching for. "No, I don't. Not in the courtroom. It would be way too distracting. The judge tends to frown on members of counsel sporting a boner. He's kind of old-fashioned like that."

A grin appeared on Cain's face, his hand sliding around to rest on Nick's hip instead. "Shame."

There was real disappointment in Cain's tone, the kind that made Nick want to keep the smiling, happy version he'd grown so attached to over the last week or so. "Maybe when I get home we can do suit *and* underwear?"

Cain made a growling noise in his throat that went straight to Nick's dick. It didn't help that Cain's fingers were skirting rather too close to his groin. He glanced at his watch, wondering if there was time for a quickie. There wasn't. Not unless he was prepared to be late on his first day back.

With that in mind, he reluctantly peeled Cain off him, already missing his body heat. He needed to take more holidays. Maybe the two of them could go away somewhere together.

Somewhere hot and isolated where they didn't have to wear many clothes and no one was around to see when the lack of clothing inevitably led to what they did best. He could picture it, a small cabin on a private beach. Nobody but the two of them. No work. No distractions.

There was a small problem with that scenario though: they still hadn't told Theo about the two of them, and he was bound to get suspicious if they both disappeared off the face of the earth at the exact same time. Cain kept pushing for them to tell him, but Nick was more cautious. What if Theo really did have an issue with his best friend and brother hooking up? Where would that leave the three of them? It might even damage his and Cain's fledgling relationship. No, it was far better to give it a bit more time, no matter how guilty he knew Cain felt about it. After all, Nick wasn't immune to the guilt—Theo was his brother. Satisfied that his tie was straight, he stepped away from the mirror. "So tonight, then? Do you want to come here or shall I come to you?"

Cain's expression turned pensive. "It's probably better if I come here. I'm working this afternoon and I'm not sure what time I'll be finished. I'll give you a call first and let you know that I'm on my way."

"You're working? Since when did the restaurant open on a Monday afternoon?"

Cain picked his jacket up off the chair where he'd left it. "It doesn't. I'm not working at the restaurant. Other work." He shrugged his arms into his jacket, fiddling with his collar when it wouldn't lie straight.

"What do you—?" Nick only got halfway through the sentence before his blood turned to ice and realization settled in his gut like a stone. He followed Cain into the living room where he was transferring his phone and wallet from the table to his pocket, seemingly oblivious to the maelstrom of emotion his simple announcement had unleashed in Nick. He stared at the back of his head, hoping that by the time Cain turned around he would have managed to shape the words flying around his head like a swarm of escaped bees into something approaching a sentence.

His body language obviously gave him away when Cain did turn, his eyes searching Nick's face. "What?"

"I didn't think you were doing that anymore?" The words were delivered far more calmly than Nick felt, nausea invading his system.

Cain's brow furrowed. "Why? We've never discussed it."

It was a valid point; they hadn't. But Nick had assumed they wouldn't need to. Was that a ridiculous assumption to have made on his part? Going by Cain's reaction, it would seem it was. "I just thought..."

Cain raised an eyebrow. "That I'd stop making porn the second your dick touched my ass." He shook his head, his face twisting into a grimace. "Sorry, that was harsh." He let out a sigh. "Look... we can talk about this, but not before this afternoon. This was booked way before we ever got together, so Evan's expecting me there to film, and I can't let him down at such short notice. So..." He shrugged as if the subject was done and dusted and his hands were tied. Like Cain had absolutely no say in what happened to his own body.

The feeling of nausea morphed into something harder with jagged edges, Nick struggling to control it. "So you're just going to go ahead and do it and I'm meant to be fine with that?"

So much for having things under control. That was the opposite of having his jealousy under control. Because that's what it was, right? It had to be. There was no other explanation for the fact that even thinking about someone else laying their hands on Cain, never mind getting anywhere near his dick made him want to tear someone limb from limb, whether it was rational or not.

Cain crossed his arms over his chest and stared steadily at Nick, his tone short and clipped when he eventually spoke. "We'll discuss it later."

Nick let out a short, sharp laugh. "After you've already fucked someone. Great! That should be a fun conversation." He forced himself to take a deep breath. "Okay, I'm just going to say it. I'm asking you not to do this. Please. Not until we've discussed it at least."

"Are you serious?" Color rose in Cain's cheeks. "You won't even tell Theo that we're in a relationship, yet you're already demanding that I quit my job."

"It wasn't a demand. It was a..." Nick couldn't even say what it was. There was no way of putting the emotions churning inside of him into words. Not without taking some time to categorize them anyway. "Is it so ridiculous that I might not be happy about my boyfriend making porn?"

Cain's eyes narrowed. "I think you need to make your mind up one way or another. I'm either your boyfriend and you need to stop keeping me a secret, because it's not just Theo, it's everyone, or I'm not your boyfriend and I can do what I want."

Nick's head was spinning. Less than five minutes ago, they'd been absolutely fine and the future had looked decidedly rosy, and now they seemed to have backed themselves into a corner. "It's only been a week." The words sounded weak even to his own ears, given that minutes earlier he'd been thinking himself that they were way farther down the relationship line than the number of days spent together would indicate. He tried one more time. "I'm just asking you not to go this afternoon. And then tonight when I get home from work, we can talk about everything, the porn, Theo, and all the people you seem to think I should have told about us."

Cain shook his head. "I'm not going to let people down just because you've decided you don't want me to do something. I may have been gaga over you for years, Nick, but that doesn't mean I'm a doormat. You can't say jump, and I say how high. That's not how relationships work between two people on an equal footing." He strode over to the door, opening it before pausing and looking back. "It's just work. I promise you that it doesn't mean a thing. I wouldn't do it if it did."

"It means something to me." Nick had barely gotten halfway through the sentence before he was talking to a closed door. He had no idea whether Cain had even heard him. If he had, then he obviously wasn't coming back to address it. How the hell had they gotten from the point where Nick was dreaming of the future to the point where the possibility they might not have one started rearing its ugly head within the space of five minutes?

He wasn't even clear on who'd fucked up. His subconscious said that it was both of them—Nick for having unrealistic expectations, and Cain for not understanding—or caring—why Nick had such a problem with it. It shouldn't have come as such a surprise really: Cain had always been strong-willed. Even as a teenager, he hadn't liked people telling him what to do.

Nick should have known that and gone about it in a different way. He really couldn't envisage it having had a different result though, even if he had. He was stupid not to have given Cain's porn career even a passing thought over the past week. Talk about an ostrich burying its head in the sand. This was real life. Not a fairy tale.

There was nothing to do except go to work. Work, and try and avoid thinking about what Cain would be getting up to that afternoon, letting someone else kiss him, touch him, fuck him. Whoever it was, he hated them. But right now, he hated Cain more. Hated him, and possibly loved him as well. Realization hit like a wrecking ball. Was that it? Love? It was certainly the only thing that seemed to fit.

Could you fall in love in just over a week? Given the amount of time they'd spent together, and the fact that he'd already known Cain, it seemed not only possible—but entirely probable. Would it make a difference to Cain? Cain had never told Nick he loved him, but he had insinuated it a couple of times. Could you be in love and then happily set off to fuck someone else, even though your boyfriend had clearly stated he wasn't happy with it? Nick had no idea. He couldn't. But then, he wasn't Cain. And Nick had always seen things as black and white more than almost anyone he knew.

One thing was clear. They needed to talk properly. He just hoped that this afternoon wouldn't do so much damage that the pieces would be impossible to put back together, and Nick could only control half of that.

EAGER FOR MORE

NICK LEANED HIS ELBOWS on his desk as he watched his phone slowly vibrate its way across his desk, the screen flashing up the name Theo. He'd spent the morning in court. Thankfully, it had been relatively straightforward, more of a scheduling hearing than an actual one. Good job, really, given how distracted he'd been, his concentration lasting no longer than a few minutes before his mind inevitably wandered back to the morning's conversation with Cain. Much as he'd tried to snap out of it, he'd found himself caught in a loop. Going by the raised eyebrows, he hadn't masked it that well either. The only saving grace was that they'd put it down to him being rusty after time off. He'd only have that excuse once though. They'd expect him to be back on top form by the following day, or tongues would start to wag. He could see the headlines now: *Nicholas Hackett loses killer edge in court.* That was probably a little too dramatic. But then, that's how he felt today.

Lunch had been spent at his desk staring at his phone while he ate a tasteless sandwich. He'd wanted to call Cain. But what could he say that he hadn't said already? He'd asked him—twice—not to do it, and it had had zero effect. He glanced at the clock—nearly two o'clock. They hadn't gotten as far as discussing what time Cain was meant to be filming; he'd just said the afternoon. But Nick guessed that it was sometime soon. *You could tell him that you're falling in love with him?* And then what? What if Cain still went ahead and filmed? Where would that leave them? No, it was better to keep that information to himself until they'd hashed everything else out. After all, Cain hadn't said he wouldn't quit. Just that he wasn't prepared to quit that afternoon. So, Nick needed to find some way of letting go of the fact that Cain was going to have someone else's tongue in his mouth that afternoon, someone else's hands on him, and someone else's cock in his ass. Easy, right? Then why did it feel like the most difficult thing in the world?

And now Theo was calling him. Nick jabbed his finger on his phone before it could go to voicemail. Ignoring Theo wasn't going to make things better. He pressed the speaker button. "Hey, little bro."

"Oh, you're alive! How come you've been off work and I've barely even spoken to you, and now that you're back at work you're suddenly available again? And don't say you've been with Bailey because his photo was splashed all over that new bar opening, and you were nowhere to be seen. Plus, I checked his Instagram. What have you been up to?"

Sleeping with your best friend, mostly. "I don't know. I've just been chilling. Everyone's always telling me I should relax more. I took their advice for once."

Theo made a sound that was half grunt and half snort. "I had no idea that hanging with your brother was so stressful. I apologize for getting in the way of your relaxation. I shall remove myself from your life forthwith. There will be no more phone calls, no more texts. I will—"

"Dick!" But Nick couldn't stop himself from smiling in spite of how miserable he'd felt all day. "You know that's not what I meant. Sorry, I should have called you."

Another grunt, followed by a sigh. "It doesn't help that it's not just you. Cain's gone to ground again as well. Have you done something else to upset him?" Theo's tone was sharp and accusatory.

Nick winced. How was he supposed to answer that? One of his reasons for avoiding Theo had been the possibility of having to tell an out-and-out lie. "Not that I'm aware of." Not unless he counted arguing with Cain about making porn. Before that, they'd been absolutely fine. "He's probably just... busy."

"Hmmm... what's up with you anyway?"

"What do you mean?"

"You sound as miserable as sin. Is it that bad being back at work? I thought you loved your job. You know Super Nick to the rescue in his continuing crusade to put all the dangerous criminals behind bars. The world's probably gone to rack and ruin while you've been gone." Theo laughed. "Is that it? Did all the criminals escape while you weren't looking? And now you've got to round them all up again."

Nick shook his head. "Have I ever told you that all those games you play give you a far too overactive imagination?"

"Multiple times." There was a pause. "So... dinner tonight to make up for ignoring me?"

Nick picked a pen up, tapping it against the table. Any other time, he would have caved immediately after Theo's carefully crafted guilt trip. But it was hardly going to help things, after the way they'd left it this morning, if he wasn't available to talk about it. Cain would think he'd done it deliberately to avoid talking to him. He'd fucked enough things up with Cain already. He couldn't afford it to be three strikes and he was out.

Cain might have been holding a torch for him for years. But that had been a fantasy, not reality. Fantasies could be a huge disappointment. The thought created a sucking pain in his chest. Was that what was going on? Cain liked Nick, but not enough to give up porn for him? He forced his mind back to the question Theo had asked him, the question he still hadn't answered. "I can't tonight."

"Why?"

He should have known Theo wouldn't let him off that easy. "There's something I've got to do. Something really important."

"And is this something a secret?"

"Yeah, kind of."

A loud sigh echoed over the phone line. "Why is everyone being so fucking weird lately?"

"Theo—"

"Forget it. Call me when you've got time for me." And then the line went dead.

Nick let his head hit the desk with a *thunk*. Great. Just when he thought things couldn't get any worse.

"Nick! Meeting's about to start. You're the only one we're waiting on."

He exhaled noisily. While Cain was fucking someone else, and Theo was probably calling him all the names under the sun, he got to listen to discussions about arraignment proceedings and deposition hearings. Fucking fantastic.

Chapter Fifteen

CAIN

Logan was still in the locker room when Cain arrived at the studio. He dropped his bag on the bench before turning to acknowledge the blond-haired man who'd already stripped down to his underwear. It had to be a blond, didn't it? It couldn't have been someone who wasn't going to remind him of Nick and make it easier. He forced himself to smile. After all, it wasn't Logan's fault that his insides were still in turmoil from that morning.

Logan sidled over to him, smiling broadly. "Hey, man."

Cain nodded in recognition of the greeting. At least the similarities between Logan and Nick ended with hair color. Logan was one of the few EagerBoyz stars who erred more on the side of twink rather than hunk with his lean and willowy physique. Evan had stated that the contrast would make them look great together on screen, and Cain agreed. Logan was cute, enthusiastic, and really easy to get along with, so Cain had been looking forward to filming a scene with him. Only, that had been before Nick. Now, when he looked at Logan, he just felt empty. He gave himself a mental shake—nerves, that's all it was. It wouldn't be the first time that it had taken him some time to settle into it and get himself in the mood. It came with the territory. Some days you were horny and up for it, and other days it really was just a job.

Cain pulled the door open on an empty locker and started stripping his shirt off, Logan hovering by his elbow.

"What do you think Evan's gonna have us do?"

Cain shrugged. He couldn't say he'd given it much thought. He'd been way too wrapped up in Nick. "No idea. The usual, I guess."

Logan leaned against the locker, moving himself into Cain's line of sight. "I've been looking forward to this. It should be good."

"Yeah, should be." Cain hoped his response sounded more convincing to Logan's ears than it did to his own.

Logan didn't pick up on his mood as he carried on with his musing of what the afternoon might hold, so it seemed he'd gotten away with it. "I reckon he'll focus on our difference in size. Maybe have you hold me up against the wall and fuck me. Blaze did that to me in our scene and it went down a storm with the subscribers. Plus, I know you don't top that much, so I reckon Evan will want to make the most of it. I mean, it's not like we could have done it the other way around. It would have looked ridiculous..."

Cain stopped listening as he shoved his shirt in the locker, toeing off his shoes before setting to work on his trousers.

"...shame you didn't dress up today. That would have made things interesting."

That got Cain's attention. So much for Blaze keeping his mouth shut. He must have been busy in the couple of weeks since Cain had last filmed. He'd probably been spreading rumors that Cain's absence was due to him attending some sort of geeky convention or something. "What's that supposed to mean?"

Logan's face fell at the sharp tone in Cain's voice. "Nothing. I didn't mean anything by it. I was just making a joke." He waved his hand up and down Cain's underwear-clad body. "I mean, look at you. I don't give a damn what you wear when you're not here."

Cain slammed the locker door shut with more force than he needed to. "What else did Blaze say?"

"Not a lot. No one cares, really. They'll give you shit because, you know, that's what we do. But what does it matter? Besides, Blaze is a dick. Everyone knows that." Logan smiled. "I have this theory that the bigger someone's dick, the bigger dick they are as a person. You know, like it's compensation or something for their personality. Look at the evidence. Angel's a dick, right? And he's got a big dick. And Blaze is an even bigger dick and he's got an even bigger—"

"Yeah, yeah. I get it." Cain cut him off, Logan's chattiness starting to grate on him, which he knew had zero to do with Logan and everything to do with how he and Nick had left things. The sooner he got this scene over and done with the better as far as he was concerned. Then he could try and work out how to tackle the mess with Nick. Because they had to be able to sort things out, right? There was no way that everything could be over and done with them in a week. Not after he'd waited ten years.

Logan trailed in his wake as they headed to the studio. He was still chatting about something, but Cain had no idea what he was saying. Evan was already in the studio, deep in conversation with Adam, the cameraman. He turned as they entered. "Hey, guys. How was the wedding, Cain?"

Trust Evan to remember that Cain had been traveling for a wedding, even though he'd only mentioned it in passing. That was one of the reasons why Evan was so popular. It probably would have been easier for him to treat them all as nothing more than cocks and holes. But he didn't. Either it was a great act, or he genuinely cared for each and every one of them as people.

That's why it was no surprise that he never had a shortage of willing applicants wanting to work for the studio. Although, Cain was probably being a bit generous there, thinking it wasn't all about sex and money. Okay, maybe Evan wasn't the reason guys joined, but he was definitely one of the reasons that most of them stuck around as long as they did.

In short, he was a good guy and not someone you ever wanted to let down. "The wedding was..." *A complete mind fuck from beginning to end.* "...good. You know, it was a wedding. Most weddings are the same—food, drink, and dancing, drunken relatives, that sort of stuff."

Turning his attention to Logan, Evan started asking him about a charity football match he'd taken part in. While everyone's attention was fixed elsewhere, Adam busy fiddling with the camera, Cain took the opportunity to arrange himself on the bed. Something didn't feel right. Like this was all some sort of dream that Cain was expecting to wake up from—a slice of normality that still felt surreal.

He scanned the room, not sure what he was expecting. Perhaps he was expecting the walls to melt away to nothing or buckle inwards. But they were the same magnolia-painted walls that they always were. Everything looked the same so he couldn't put his finger on what had changed.

The bed gave as Logan joined him on it, Evan pulling his chair into the usual position at the foot of the bed as he straddled it, the countdown to filming starting as Evan launched into his usual quick rundown of what he wanted to see.

"...make the most of Cain topping for once, so we'll start on the bed and then we'll do some filming against the wall with Cain holding you up."

Logan wore a big grin on his face as he nudged Cain. "Told you so." He was almost vibrating with excitement. In contrast, Cain still felt nothing.

"...then usual stuff. We'll end in missionary so that we can get facial expressions for both cum shots. You've both been here long enough to know what you're doing. So you know the drill, follow the structure of what I've said, but where you know improvisation will be hot, go for it." He clapped his hands together, Cain startling at the noise. "Right! Let's get this show on the road."

Logan pushed Cain onto his back, wasting no time in jumping on top of him, his lips descending towards Cain's. A bolt of sheer panic hit him in the chest. This wasn't right. They looked nothing like Nick's lips. Wrong shape. Wrong shade of pink. Wrong everything. And they wouldn't feel the same either. He knew that would be the case even before they touched his.

Snapshots of that morning jumped into his head. *Is it so ridiculous that I might not be happy about my boyfriend making porn? I'm asking you not to do this. Please. It means something to me.* What the hell was he thinking? He'd wanted Nick for years. He finally had him in his grasp, and he was throwing it all away. For what? Money? Just to be stubborn? Out of a twisted sense of loyalty to Evan? He didn't even know anymore. All he knew was that what he was about to do felt more wrong than anything ever had before. That's what had changed. Not the room, him. He was different. Nausea rose inside Cain as Logan's lips touched his when all he could see was Nick's face.

He wrenched his head away and shoved at Logan's chest, the unexpected action causing Logan to topple sideways. Cain scrambled off the bed, needing to put as much distance between himself and the blond twink as he could. That left him standing in the middle of the room, his heart pounding as three pairs of eyes stared at him with equally shocked expressions on their face. Cain needed to say something. But what? His brain was a mess, so how was he supposed to explain it to someone else.

It was Evan who seemed to recover first, or at least he was the first to find his voice. "Everything alright, Cain?"

Cain almost laughed. It was such a stupid question, but typical Evan, able to remain calm amid the storm of others' irrational behavior. "I can't do this! I'm sorry."

Evan inclined his head toward the door to the exit. "Let's talk outside." He offered a reassuring smile and a wink in Logan's direction.

Cain had no idea how Logan had responded because he couldn't bring himself to even look in his direction. If the guys had been having so much fun with him being a secret geek, then they were going to love this one. They'd probably find some way of linking the two things together.

He preceded Evan out of the room, leaning back against the wall in the corridor, the brickwork cool against his bare skin. Evan closed the door as he joined him, his expression exuding nothing but concern. "What's going on, Cain? I never expected you of all people to pull the frightened rabbit act. I've had that from newbies before, but not someone who's already filmed dozens of scenes for me."

It would have been easier if Evan had been angry at him. Evan *should* be angry at him. Why wasn't he? Did he think he was going to be able to talk Cain into going back in there? Cain exhaled slowly, trying to work out how to put what he was feeling into words. But his brain was still jumbled. All he knew was that he didn't want to be there. That he shouldn't be there. Not when it didn't feel right and Nick had expressly asked him not to do it.

In the face of Cain's continued silence, Evan started aiming questions at him. "Are you ill?"

Cain shook his head.

"Has something happened? Something that's on your mind?"

"Sort of."

Feeling guilty for standing there like a lumbering idiot and making Evan do all the work, Cain made another attempt to translate some of his anxiety into words. It was the very least that he owed Evan. "I have a... a Nick."

Evan's brow furrowed. "A... what?"

"Nick!" Cain was doing a fantastic job of this. He glanced back at the door, half expecting to see Logan and Adam having appeared as a pair of interested spectators—God knows he would have wanted to know what was going on if the shoe had been on the other foot—but the door was still closed. "I've been seeing someone. His name is Nick."

Comprehension dawned on Evan's face. "Ah, right! Nick is a person." He tilted his head to one side, still demonstrating the same steadfast patience. "Tell me about Nick."

The dam broke and Cain suddenly went from not being able to say anything to it all spilling out at once. "He's my friend's brother. Not just a friend. My best friend. I've had a crush on him for years… Nick… that is, not Theo. I could never look at Theo like that. But Nick never looked at me twice. Not until the party a few weeks back when he discovered I made porn because I hadn't told anyone. He was horrified, at least I think so. Maybe it was just shock. But there was something else about the way he was looking at me, so I tried to kiss him. He ran away. Then at the wedding he ran away again, but then we had sex, and he apologized for what had happened at the wedding. Not the sex. Something else. And the last ten days has been great. Until this morning when he found out I was coming here and we had an argument, and Nick got upset, and he probably won't even speak to me because I was far too stubborn and I refused to listen to him because I'm an idiot and I don't really like being told what to do. But that's what happens in relationships, right? You argue and then you make up and work out how you can put things right. I guess I've still got a lot to learn… and… yeah, that's kind of where I am at the moment."

Evan blinked a few times as if he was trying to ward off the avalanche of information that had just flown his way at rapid speed. He shifted so that he was on the same side of the corridor as Cain, lifting one arm to lean against the wall by his side. "Nick was the one at the party, right? The one who looked as if he couldn't decide whether he'd wandered into a hellhole, or a candy shop?"

Cain laughed at the almost perfect description. He really had looked like that. "Yeah, that was Nick."

"And you and he are a couple now?"

It was one of those questions that should have been easy to answer, and no doubt if someone had asked him before that morning, he would have said yes without hesitation. But things seemed a lot more complex now, so all he could do was be honest. "I don't know. I thought we were, but it's only been just over a week. And Theo still doesn't know about us. So..." He left the sentence unfinished.

"But he doesn't want you making porn?"

Cain shook his head. "Not according to how he reacted this morning when he found out I was coming here."

Evan's gaze fastened on Cain's face. "And what about you? What do you want?"

Cain considered the question before he answered it. "I thought I wanted my life to carry on the same way as it was. But then when it came down to it, in there with Logan, I just... all I wanted was Nick. It felt all wrong. Does that make sense?" He wasn't expecting the broad smile that took up residence on Evan's face. The man was meant to be annoyed at him, not grinning at him like an idiot. "What?"

Evan raised an eyebrow. "It's just funny, that's all. He doesn't want you to make porn, and you don't want to make it. The two of you are in absolute agreement, then, so I'm not quite sure why you seem to be having such an existential crisis about it. It seems pretty simple to me. So I guess this is you quitting?"

Cain couldn't believe it could be that easy. "Can I do that? I don't need to work some sort of notice period?" He frowned as Evan immediately started laughing.

"This is porn, not a secretarial job. I can't tell you that you need to continue having sex against your will for a few weeks. I'm a porn producer, not a pimp. If you want to quit, consider yourself as having quit with immediate effect. You can always come back if things don't work out and I'll welcome you with open arms. Just make sure that whatever you do, it's *your* decision and not one you're making because you feel you have to. Relationships where one person sacrifices everything for the other don't usually have a happy ending."

Evan's advice made a lot of sense. Cain thought back over everything that had happened over the last few weeks. Was it really his decision, or was he caving to emotional bribery? But there was no getting past the truth of how he'd felt in the studio. He'd had zero interest in having sex with Logan. And there was absolutely nothing wrong with Logan. Far from it. He cast his mind over the entire EagerBoyz roster. He suddenly couldn't imagine having sex with any of them. Yeah, the only thing it had to do with Nick was the fact that he was head over heels in love with him. "It's definitely my decision. I just wish I'd made it a few hours ago." He eyed Evan's relaxed body language. "I do think you should be a lot more annoyed at me. I just wrecked your scene."

The other man shrugged. "Does it help if I tell you that I won't be paying you for this afternoon, and that as I'll have to pay Adam and Logan anyway for their time, I'll be taking that payment from any money I owe you? My time, however, you can have for free."

"Sounds fair." It sounded more than fair and Cain was grateful. "You're a really nice guy, Evan. Which begs the question why you're single?"

Evan let out a short, sharp laugh. "Are you serious? Maybe it's because I spend all my time here, hanging out with guys young enough to be my son. And even if they weren't, or that didn't matter and I was ever tempted, it's definitely hands-off territory."

There was a far-away look in Evan's eyes that seemed to suggest that the temptation he'd mentioned might not be as rhetorical as he was making it sound. Cain wondered if there was a story lurking there somewhere, and if so who might have caught Evan's eye. It was none of his business though, and the last thing he wanted to do with Evan being so understanding was come across as nosy. Besides, he was suddenly aware of the fact that all of his soul baring had taken place in just his underwear. He gestured in the direction of the locker room. "I should..."

Evan nodded, his eyes twinkling. "Yeah, good idea. And then I suggest you go and find your boyfriend and sort things out between the two of you. Good luck. Let me know how it goes."

Cain made a dash for the locker room, skidding to a halt at the end of the corridor as something suddenly occurred to him. He spun around to find Evan in the exact same spot he'd left him. "Can you apologize to Logan for me? Tell him it had absolutely nothing to do with him." He waited for Evan's nod before continuing on his way.

Within five minutes, he was already halfway to his car. He wanted to talk to Nick. No, scrap that, he *needed* to talk to

Nick. The only problem was that Nick would still be at work, so he'd have to wait. His heart leapt into his throat as his phone vibrated with a text. Was that him? Was Nick feeling just as bad about things as he was? The optimism lasted only as long as it took him to read Theo's name on the screen.

Theo: *I don't know if you remember me. We went to school together. I was the boy who used to carry your books for you back when you were still skinny and no one could see you when you stood sideways. I can totally understand if you don't remember me, seeing as it's been so long since we last saw each other. I've cried. The game console has cried. I used to have a brother too, but he no longer makes time for me either.*

Signed, your very old friend, Theo, who has no one to play with, but it's fine. It's absolutely fine. I'll just fill a bath with my tears and take up writing sad poetry.

Cain: *You're such a drama queen. Are you sure you're not gay?*

Theo: *Oh my God! Cain's talking to me. My prayers have been answered. Hang on. Let me bring up a picture of Charlize Theron. Yep. Pretty sure I'm still straight. What are you up to? PLEASE tell me you can come round tonight?*

Cain stared at his watch. There was still two hours until Nick got off work, and that was assuming he left on time, which he knew wasn't always the case. The world of restaurants and law were very different places. And it wasn't as if he'd been planning on hanging around Nick's workplace like a sad puppy in order to speak to him the very second he left work. He had plenty of time to go over to Theo's, make up for being such a bad friend, and then get Nick to talk to him.

Cain: *I could come round now for a couple of hours, but I have to go somewhere important this evening, so you can't try and play the* "emotional bribery you have to stay" *card.*

The next message was a selfie of Theo wearing an overly exaggerated shocked expression. His friend was a doofus but Cain loved him for it.

Theo: *Me? I think you're mixing me up with some other incredibly good-looking young man who also goes by the name of Theo. I wouldn't dream of doing such a thing. I don't even know what the words emotional bribery mean.*

Cain rolled his eyes. Despite the sob story, Theo was obviously in a good mood. It was probably exactly what he needed to distract him from the coming showdown with Nick.

Chapter Sixteen

NICK

Nick swore at his phone, barely resisting the urge to kick something. As he was still standing in the doorway of the offices where he worked, it probably wasn't the best idea though. His plan to leave work early and find Cain had already been derailed by the fact that Cain wasn't picking up his phone. He tried again with the exact same result, the phone ringing and ringing before going to voicemail.

As Nick wasn't even sure what he was going to say face to face to Cain, never mind in a message, he hung up. Was Cain still filming? He didn't have a clue how long it took. Why would he? He'd never had any reason to look into it. All he knew was that he needed to speak to Cain. Preferably tonight so that he might be capable of keeping his mind on his job the following day.

What was he going to say to Cain? He needed advice and he needed it fast. There was only one person he could think of that could be trusted to give him the absolute unvarnished truth without worrying about hurting Nick's feelings. He dialed the number, Bailey picking up just before Nick was about to face another recorded message, his voice decidedly breathless. "This better be important."

Nick stepped out of the doorway and began to make his way down the street. He didn't need any busybody colleagues listening in on their way out of the building. "It *is* important."

"So you're not just calling me for relationship advice, then?"

Busted! "Since when are relationships not important?" He didn't need to see Bailey to know that he was rolling his eyes on the other end of the phone. Bailey was the most anti-relationship person Nick knew, but he still had a way of managing to cut through the bullshit and get to the crux of the matter. He needed Bailey to help him put things into perspective so that when he tracked Cain down, he didn't fuck things up.

"Five minutes. That's all you've got. I've got men in my bed waiting for me."

Nick stuck his arm out to hail a passing cab, climbing into the back once the driver had pulled up to the curb. He slammed the door shut and settled back on the seat. "So... Cain and I made up after I was a dick to him at the wedding."

"I figured as much seeing as I've barely had more than the odd text from you since. Did the two of you manage to surface from bed at all?"

A reluctant smile pulled at the edges of Nick's lips. "Sometimes. When we had to eat."

"So... what have you done now?"

Nick leaned his head back against the seat and sighed. "I didn't realize that he still intended on making porn. We hadn't discussed it, and I guess I'd just assumed that if we were in a relationship that he would stop. He was meant to be filming a scene this afternoon. When he told me, I made it clear that I wasn't very happy and asked him not to. Which in retrospect wasn't a very good approach to take with Cain. I know him better than that. Anyway, to cut a long story short, he made it clear he was still going to go ahead with it, and we didn't leave things on a very good note. And now I'm not sure how to resolve it. So I need your blunt advice. You know, the type you always give me because you're missing that part that worries about hurting my feelings."

Bailey let out a little snort. "Too right. It's the only reason you keep me around. That and all the free drinks I put your way. But, listen..." He cleared his throat and Nick steeled himself for Bailey's assessment of the situation. "You've been together, what? A week? Ten days? It's not that long. What makes you think you can dictate his life choices after a week?" Nick opened his mouth to interject but Bailey hadn't finished. "You knew when you slept with him for the first time that he made porn. Therefore, nothing about *him* has changed, only your reading of the situation. You need to make your mind up, Nick, whether you'll accept him just as he is, or whether it's something you can't get over. Because, my friend, I shouldn't need to tell you of all people that expecting someone to change for you is utter crap. Did it work for you when you had boyfriends who asked you not to wear the underwear?"

"That's different."

"Maybe." Bailey sniffed. "Maybe not." There was a pause as if he was shifting the phone from one ear to the other. "You either like Cain or you don't."

"You make it sound so simple."

"It's as complicated as you want to make it. You can tie yourself up in knots over Cain having sex with someone else. Sex which probably means less than nothing to him, and throw away a good thing, or you can try and find some way of accepting it, accepting him." Bailey sighed. "I probably am oversimplifying it, but, you know, there needs to be give and take in every relationship, or so I hear from those people who are crazy enough to get sucked into one. Right, can I go now?"

Nick shook his head in amusement. "You'll meet someone one day, and you'll eat your words."

"Doubtful. They'd have to catch me first. I've gotta go. I've got far better things to be doing than talking to you."

Something suddenly dawned on Nick, a snippet of the conversation from earlier that hadn't registered at the time. "Hang on! Did you say *men* in your bed, as in plural? Not man? What's going on, Bailey?" But he was already listening to dead air, Bailey having hung up on him. Had he misheard? He was still staring at his phone when a text came through.

Theo: *I found a replacement for tonight, just in case any guilt happened to creep in about your poor, lonely brother.*

It was closely followed by a picture of a familiar dark head bent over a game console. Well, that answered one question—Cain's location. Nick leaned forward, sliding the glass partition back that separated him from the driver. "Change of plan. I've got a new address for you."

NICK HAD IT ALL PLANNED out in his head by the time the cab dropped him off outside Theo's house. So much so that even he couldn't believe how he'd acted that morning. Who the hell had he thought he was, deciding Cain's future for him? The only excuse he had was that the two of them had been so wrapped up in each other for the past week that real life had seemed like some strange concept, and Cain's announcement had been like someone sticking a very sharp pin into the fantasy world they'd constructed. Only, it didn't have to be a fantasy, did it? They just needed to find a balance between the two. As Bailey had pointed out, Nick just needed to decide what was important to him. Well, he'd decided, and he was eager to let the man himself know. He didn't bother to knock, fumbling the spare key from out of his pocket and letting himself in.

"Son of a bitch!"

He smiled as the familiar voice rang out, following the sound into the living room where Cain was sprawled across a beanbag, his fingers hammering at the Xbox controller while his gaze was fastened on the TV, his avatar currently being set upon by a horde of trolls. Cain slammed the controller down as the words "Game over" flashed up on the screen. "Motherfucking troll dickheads!"

"Did the trolls win?"

Cain's head whipped around so fast that he almost toppled off the beanbag. He stared at Nick open-mouthed as if he was trying to work out where he'd suddenly appeared from. He dropped the controller on the floor and clambered slowly to his feet without taking his eyes off Nick.

Nick wasn't doing much better. He found himself studying Cain, taking in everything from the dark hair that fell over his brow to the body he now knew so well. Cain's brown eyes held a mixture of confusion and trepidation. Nick had butterflies, yet another piece of evidence of how much Cain mattered to him. Somewhere along the line, friendship and lust had blended into something much stronger and much deeper, with plenty of scope for it to go deeper still. At least, it could if he didn't manage to fuck this up. He took a deep breath, running back through the speech he'd practiced in the cab after discovering Cain's whereabouts.

"Hey! I've been trying to call you. Quite a few times."

Cain's hand dipped into his pocket, pulling out his phone and frowning at it. How many times had he called him? Five? Six? More? Cain flicked the switch on the side before lifting his head. "Sorry. It was on silent and I didn't feel it vibrate." He lifted an arm to point in the direction of the TV screen as if that explained everything. "I was going to call you once I knew you were out of work. Listen, Nick..."

Nick held a hand up to stall him. "No, I need to say something first. I was wrong this morning and you were right. I can't just decide things for both of us. That's not fair. I was stupid to think that you were going to give up porn just like that, and just because I'd asked. It was..." He shook his head, trying to choose his words carefully. Practiced speeches were all very well, but it wasn't like he'd made cue cards. "...unrealistic of me. It would have been different if we'd discussed it. I don't know why it hadn't occurred to me. Maybe because I was still struggling to get my head around it. I remember you as a skinny fourteen-year-old kid and I never would have predicted that same fourteen-year-old would have ended up making porn. Not that there's anything wrong with it." Nick cursed himself internally. His speech seemed to be going to hell in a handbasket. Nobody would ever believe that words were his thing in a courtroom. But then, none of the cases he'd ever worked mattered as much as this did. No wonder Cain was staring at him in a way that said he wasn't sure what he was supposed to say.

Nick swallowed and tried again. "What I'm trying to say is… and I know I'm making a real hash of it… I don't care what you did this afternoon. If you tell me that it's just work, then I have absolutely no reason to doubt that. I should be mature enough to cope with feelings of jealousy without turning into a caveman."

"You were jealous?"

Why did Cain sound so surprised? "Of course I was. Wasn't it obvious? The thought of someone else getting to touch you… to… well, you know… it made me completely irrational. But I can get past that for the sake of our relationship, assuming we still have one and I haven't screwed everything up? I want what we've had for the past week to carry on."

The seconds that passed as he waited for Cain's response seemed far longer in Nick's mind. Finally, the corners of Cain's mouth twitched up into a semi-grin. "So what you're saying is, you'll take me warts and all, and you'd even be fine, with occasional moments of badly hidden jealousy, with me continuing to work for EagerBoyz?"

Nick nodded, suddenly finding his arms full of muscular hunk. He buried his nose in Cain's hair, breathing in the familiar scent as his arms tightened around his boyfriend's waist, the label causing him to have to hide a smile. Because there was no getting past it anymore, was there? Their relationship might have started off one-sided, but it had rapidly adjusted to the point where there were feelings on both sides. Maybe it was Cain's easy acceptance of Nick's kink, or perhaps it was because they'd already been friends. He didn't know, and to be honest he didn't want to waste time analyzing it. It would be far more sensible to switch off the lawyer part of his brain and simply enjoy. Concentrate on the present, rather than the past, or the future. He turned his head slightly to the side so his voice wouldn't be muffled when he spoke. "Does that mean you forgive me?"

Cain pulled back slightly. "Yeah, I forgive you. I could have handled it better myself, and it wasn't that I deliberately hadn't mentioned it to you. I just hadn't given it a thought." A sudden urgency blossomed on his face. "I need to tell you something though. Something important."

Nick's heart did a little flip, the butterflies back with a vengeance, and the trepidation he felt reflected in his voice. "What?"

"I didn't do it."

Cain's statement made very little sense. "Didn't do what?"

"This afternoon... I went there... I was going to do it, but then when it came down to it, I couldn't."

A lightbulb flicked on in Nick's head. He tried to fight down the giddying sense of relief that threatened to overwhelm him, worried that it would make him a hypocrite after everything he'd said. "Why not?"

Cain smiled, his fingers gripping on to Nick's shoulders. "When it came down to it, I didn't want to kiss anyone that wasn't you. I certainly didn't want to do more than that. I quit. I'm not doing it anymore."

"So..." Nick's head was spinning. "You just let me deliver a whole speech about how I was absolutely fine with you making porn when you'd already quit."

"Yeah, but don't you see." Cain's hand moved to cup Nick's neck, his thumb softly stroking along his jawline. "The fact that you said you could look past it means the world to me. It shows me you actually care, and that you're in it for the long haul. Not just for a few weeks or until something better comes along."

Nick took exception to that last comment. "How could you think that?" He gave himself a moment to think about it, conceding that perhaps Cain had a point. "Okay, maybe before last week. But we've spent nearly every minute together in the last ten days. What did I do to give you that impression? Tell me so I don't do it again."

Cain shook his head ruefully. "You didn't. I just... you know it's hard to pine for someone for years and then get your head around the fact that I might have actually gotten what I wanted. It's gonna take some time to get used to it." His smile turned seductive. "I mean, being extra attentive would help." Cain's other hand slid up Nick's chest before settling on the opposite side of Nick's neck to mirror the first, his lips closing over Nick's seconds later.

Nick put everything he had into that kiss, wanting it to be a fresh start, a promise, and anything else he could make it, all at the same time. Maybe arguing wasn't so bad if making up felt like this. He let his hands roam over Cain's muscular back, already starting to anticipate getting rid of the infuriating folds of fabric that were preventing him from getting to bare skin.

"Fuck me!"

For a moment, Nick was sure the words had come from Cain. So much so that the response of "with pleasure" was on the tip of his tongue, and he was already contemplating whether there was a condom in his wallet. Only for it to register that Cain's tongue was in his mouth. Cain was clever, but not that clever.

Nick wrenched his head away and met Theo's shocked gaze, his younger brother staring at the two of them as if he'd just walked in on his parents having sex. Nick glared at him, his throbbing cock, which was pressed against Cain's thigh, not allowing him to think past the fact that his plans for the next few minutes had suddenly been thwarted. "What are you doing here?"

Nick's glare was returned with interest. "What am *I* doing here? I live here. What the fuck are you doing here when you said you were busy? And what's"—Theo flapped his hands in the general direction of Cain, his face twisting into a grimace—"this touching, kissing thing about?"

Right! They were in Theo's living room. Somehow in all the rush to salvage his and Cain's fledgling relationship, Nick had managed to forget that one crucial fact. So had Cain apparently, who seemed to have been struck dumb.

Theo's gaze flicked between the two of them. "Can someone please tell me what's going on? I leave Cain alone for two minutes to go and make a phone call and I come back to find my brother and my best friend sucking each other's faces, which I've got to tell you is really gross. God knows what you'd have been up to if I'd been a few minutes longer. I could have been mentally scarred. And neither of you are talking. Start talking."

Nick glanced Cain's way, hoping for help, but as Cain didn't look any closer to being able to speak, he guessed it was down to him. Well, Cain had wanted Theo to know—not like this maybe, neither of them had wanted it to happen like this—but it seemed he was going to get his wish. "We've kind of been seeing each other."

"Kind of?"

The question had come from Cain rather than his brother. At least he'd found his voice, even if it was only to question Nick. He shot him a look of apology. There was no way that he wanted to risk undoing all the good work he'd just done. He squared his shoulders, looking his brother straight in the eye. "Correction. We've been seeing each other."

Theo sank into a chair. "Since when?"

"The wedding?" Nick flicked another glance in Cain's direction. It was like taking part in the strangest quiz show imaginable where he only won a prize if he managed to answer without alienating either of the two men who were so important to him. Cain nodded and Nick imagined a point being added to an imaginary scoreboard.

"The wedding!" Theo's eyes blazed as he turned his attention to Cain. "Oh my God! Did you steal the spare room key so you could go and fuck my brother? That's... ugh... I don't even know what that is."

The accusation finally managed to shake Cain from his vow of silence. "It wasn't like that. I told you the truth. I went there with the intention of giving him a piece of my mind, but..." He stopped talking, his cheeks turning a lovely shade of pink as both of them recalled exactly what had happened.

It was funny to think that a little over a week ago Nick had been concerned that Cain might divulge his secret. Now he was a hundred percent positive that no matter how close Theo and Cain might be, those words would never leave Cain's lips.

Cain continued. "Well, you don't need to know the details, but, yeah, things happened."

Theo waved his hands in the direction of the spot where they'd been standing when he'd entered the room. "I didn't need to see *that*, but you forced me to watch it."

"Theo?" Nick intended on telling his brother that for once the extra dose of drama really wasn't needed, that it wouldn't help anything, but Cain got there first.

"I don't know why you're so shocked by this. You of all people know how I've felt about your brother... for years."

"Yeah, but"—Theo screwed his face up—"I didn't think he would ever return those feelings." His accusing glance ricocheted back to Nick. "Hang on! What are you playing at?" His voice rose to a shrill pitch. "Are you messing my friend about and using him for sex? Because if you are..."

Nick quirked an eyebrow, starting to see the funny side of the conversation. "If I am, you'll what? Set Mum and Dad on me? Give me a good telling off?" Cain's fingers curling around his forearm served as a warning to not go too far. Nick shifted his arm, interlocking their fingers so he could hold Cain's hand instead. After all, what better time to present a united front. The secret was out; they didn't need to hide anything anymore. "I'm not using him. I wouldn't do that, so you don't need to go all protective friend on my ass. This is going to be a long-term thing, so you're going to have to get used to it, one way or the other."

Theo's gaze flicked to Cain's face, seeking confirmation. His indignant body language deflated somewhat as Cain nodded. "I see. Well, I guess that explains why I haven't been able to get hold of both of you for the last week or so."

This time the accusing stare encompassed both of them. From the way Cain's fingers tightened in his, Nick surmised that he felt just as guilty as he did. "I'm not going to steal him away from you. We were just... you know, everything was new."

"Oh, great. So you're going to get bored of me?" Cain let go of Nick's hand and crossed his arms over his chest, his eyebrow raised.

Back to the quiz show again, except this time he'd lost a point. It reminded him that he'd never been able to handle the two of them together. He guessed he was going to have to learn. "No, that's not what I meant. I just meant..." Hell, he didn't even know what he meant. He shook his head. "Can't we just agree to handle this like the adults that we are?"

Theo pulled a face. "Sure, we can. I just need to get over the fact that the two of you have been keeping secrets from me, and bleach my eyeballs to get rid of that lovely little making-out show that you put on for me in my own home. Then we'll all be fine and dandy." He plonked himself on the beanbag Cain had vacated and picked up the controller. "I'm going to kill some trolls. Less chance of them being caught in an embrace. Don't screw in my bed!"

Nick bit his lip to keep from smiling. Despite Theo's prickly exterior, he could have taken it far worse. It might take some time to sand off the sharp edges and work a few things out between them, but they'd get there given time. He grabbed Cain's hand and tugged him in the direction of the kitchen. "We'll make a cup of tea. Maybe some food."

Theo grunted, still having the presence of mind to call after them, despite the game having started. "Stay away from my bedroom. I'm serious."

Chuckling, Nick closed the kitchen door before pulling an unresisting Cain back into his arms. "Now, where were we?"

Cain gave his chest a mock shove but there wasn't any real strength or intent to it, a heat already manifesting in his eyes. "You do realize that Theo will skin us both alive if he catches us at it again. We need to give him some time to get used to it. At least he knows now, though."

Nick nodded. All in all, it had been a rather long and trying day. He rested his chin on top of Cain's head, feeling strangely at peace with the world. It seemed like the perfect time to let go of the words that had been foremost in his mind all day. "You should probably know that I'm falling for you."

Cain pulled back, his eyes searching Nick's face as if he thought it could be some sort of horrific prank that Nick was pulling. Nick met his gaze steadily. Finally, Cain relaxed. "Good. Because you already know that I've fallen for you. It's about time you caught up." His hands plucked at Nick's lapels, his tongue darting out to moisten his bottom lip. "You're so fucking hot in a suit."

"Yeah?" Nick slid his thigh between Cain's, fitting their bodies together perfectly. "What about Theo?"

"Theo's average time on this game is about ten minutes, so by my calculations we've got eight left."

Nick dipped his head, brushing his lips over Cain's in a barely there caress. "What kind of person times games so that they know how long the average one is?"

Cain winked. "Geeks, Nick. That's who. It comes with the territory. The good news is that I only time games, nothing else."

"Thank fuck for that!"

"They—"

But Nick had already moved in for a kiss, cutting off whatever it was Cain had been going to say. He had no intention of wasting the next seven minutes.

Epilogue

CAIN

The trail of clothes strewn across the floor told its own story. Cain followed it with his eyes, starting at the tie dangling from the door handle. From there it was suit jacket, shirt, trousers, socks and then finally a tiny scrap of white lace that Cain had removed with his teeth. The underwear thing was rarer now. Partly because Nick was guaranteed to bust so fast when anything lacy or silky was involved and partly because it took preparation, and quite frankly Cain couldn't always wait to pounce on his boyfriend or vice versa.

"Are you dressing me with your eyes?"

Cain snorted, rolling onto his side, and propping himself up on his elbow so that he could see Nick's face properly. He let his fingers do the talking, tracing the contours of Nick's chest and watching the skin pebble beneath his fingertips. "Possibly... although I like the naked version as well."

Nick raised an eyebrow. "Like?"

Cain let his fingers explore lower, brushing a finger over one of Nick's nipples. "Are you fishing for declarations of love?"

"Maybe." Nick might have said maybe, but the smile playing on his lips said definitely.

Cain squirmed across the bed so that he could drape himself across Nick's chest, his chin resting on his hands as he stared into Nick's eyes. "I love you, Nicholas Peter Hackett. I think I have since I was fourteen and I expect I will for many more years to come."

Nick tilted his head to one side. "What do you love about me?"

Cain pretended to consider it. This wasn't the first time they'd played this game. "I love... your suits. I love your..." Inspiration suddenly struck. "I love your coffee machine because it's so much faster than mine." He stifled a smile at the unimpressed look on Nick's face. "I love your shower for similar reasons to the coffee machine. I love your..." Nick sighed dramatically, the action jolting Cain's precarious position. He managed to right himself, letting the rest of the words out in a rush. "Then of course there's your face and your body." He pressed his hands over Nick's heart. "And not forgetting all those other wonderful qualities you have like the fact that you always wake me up to say goodbye in the morning before you leave for work, and the massages you give me when I've had a difficult shift at the restaurant." He lifted his hand and dropped a kiss in the exact same spot. "I love everything about you."

Nick threaded a hand in Cain's hair encouraging him closer, his eyes already saying what his lips were about to. "I love you too."

Cain smiled, his stomach flipping like he was on a roller coaster. Nick might have been saying it for weeks, but he never got tired of hearing it, and he doubted he ever would. Each and every time sent the same mixture of warmth and tingles coursing through him. He had no idea how he'd ever gotten this lucky. A few months ago, he'd been lucky to grab Nick's attention for more than five minutes at a time. Now he had his undivided attention. And it was glorious in every way. He dropped a lingering kiss on Nick's lips before raising his head. "Don't let Theo hear you say that."

The groan Nick gave in response was expected. Theo was still putting them both through the mill, as only a best friend or sibling could get away with. They'd almost had to draw up a rota in order to keep him happy, and woe betide if either of them went more than a couple of days without contacting him. They'd tried dinners with the three of them, but it was difficult to enjoy your food when someone was sitting in the corner making comments if your fingers happened to brush or you looked at the other one too lovingly. It was like trying to take a toddler out to eat.

Sighing, Nick rolled them both onto their sides, his thigh fitting between Cain's. "We need to find him a girlfriend so he's not as needy."

"Can't you get one of your model contacts to date him?"

Nick quirked an eyebrow. "I am many things, but I'm not a magician. This is Theo we're talking about. The date would be fine until he opened his mouth and started telling them about the best way to kill the boss on level eighteen of some game he's been playing."

Cain smirked. It was so accurate he could picture it happening. The poor model would probably be forced to climb out the bathroom window in order to escape. "You put up with me."

Nick rolled his eyes. "Yeah, but I've learnt numerous ways to shut you up."

"And there I was thinking you just really liked blow jobs."

"That's just an added bonus."

They both turned their heads towards the nightstand as Cain's phone vibrated with a message. Nick made a huffing sound. "That's probably him now. You better reply before he starts telling us that neither of us loves him anymore *again*."

Cain twisted around, managing to grapple his phone without disengaging from Nick. He held it above his head while he read the message which wasn't from Theo. "It's from Evan. There's an EagerBoyz get-together next week and he wants to know if I'm interested in going. Would that bother you?" He studied Nick's face, searching for any evidence of Nick saying one thing but meaning another. He'd been touched when Evan had kept in contact. They'd even had coffee together a couple of times, and it wasn't because Evan had been trying to lure him back to the studio, because he'd never mentioned it. Unless it was the most covert plan in the history of covert plans. He'd even told Cain that once he was a part of the family, he stayed a part of the family whether he'd liked it or not. Cain had choked on his coffee at that point thinking that it had to be the most dysfunctional family ever where they all screwed each other. But he appreciated the sentiment, and it would be kind of fun to see everyone again.

Nick's expression remained neutral. "What day?"

"Thursday."

"That could work out well because Bailey's been nagging me to go to a gallery opening with him on Thursday." Nick paused. "Don't pull that face when I mention Bailey's name."

Cain couldn't help himself. It wasn't for the reason he used to pull faces when it came to Bailey. He was one hundred percent sure that Bailey wasn't remotely interested in Nick. Sure, he flirted. But from what he'd seen of Bailey, he'd flirt with a lamppost if it happened to be in his path. He just couldn't work the man out. He was too spontaneous, too impulsive, and so carefree that any time spent in Bailey's company made Cain's head spin. "You know how I feel about him. I just don't get him, and I find it weird that the two of you are friends. He's like your total opposite."

Nick did his best impression of a shrug while lying down. "I won't go if you have a problem with it?"

"And I won't go to the EagerBoyz party if you have a problem with me hanging out with them?"

They stared at each other for a moment before both breaking into simultaneous grins. They'd come a long way since their first argument when neither of them had been prepared to budge an inch. There'd been wrinkles along the way but they'd finally reached the point where they both recognized that the most important thing was consideration of the other. Cain felt like someone should be coming in to hand him a certificate which said *"all grown up"* on the front.

Nick flicked him on the nose. "Well, that's that sorted. Now the only problem is which one of us is going to take Theo so that we can keep the rest of the nights next week to ourselves?"

Cain gave it all of a second's consideration. "You should take him."

Nick winced. "Last time I took him to a gallery he got drunk and threw up in a plant pot."

"I can't take him to hang out with a load of gay porn stars. Remember your face at that party and then multiply it by ten."

The grin on Nick's face was decidedly evil. "Oh, go on. And take photos. Tell him that there might be some female porn stars there, and then you can just pretend that they couldn't make it. Just think about how much of a pain he's been lately. It would serve him right to suffer a little bit."

He had a point. It would definitely pay Theo back for milking every last bit of guilt that he could from the two of them. If he told Cain one more time that it was the keeping secrets from him that had been the hardest part to get over, Cain wouldn't be responsible for his actions. "You know, some people would find it weird that you want me to take your straight little brother to a gay porn party."

Nick had now perfected the supine shrug. He held his hand out. "Do we have a deal?"

Although post-sex handshakes seemed a little too formal, Cain took it anyway. When he tried to take his hand back, Nick refused to let go, dragging Cain with him toward the edge of the bed. "Shower time."

Cain made a pathetic attempt to resist. "You could shower on your own."

Nick shook his head. "That's no fun." He stuck his bottom lip out in a pout which Cain was pretty sure he'd learnt from Bailey. It certainly wasn't something he'd picked up in the courtroom. "Please."

Rolling his eyes, Cain let himself be led into the shower cubicle. He might have made a comment about Nick's shower being better earlier but it was a tight squeeze for the two of them. And the problem was they kept trying to have sex in there when it really wasn't big enough. A pattern that kept resulting in failure. "You need to get a bigger shower."

"I will when you move in."

Cain tipped his head back under the hot water. "I thought I already had."

"Not officially."

His cock started to take an interest in proceedings as Nick's warm hands soaped every inch of his body. "What would make it official?"

"Giving up your own place and *all* your things being here."

Cain squirmed as Nick started to nuzzle his neck. He wanted that. He wanted it more than he wanted anything. But there was something else he wanted and he had to find his opportunities where he could. "On one condition."

Nick lined their cocks up, the soapy water making it easier for them to slide together. "Name it."

"You come to Comic Con with me and Theo. *And* you dress up."

Nick's eyes were soft as he stared into Cain's. "You don't have to bribe me. If you want me there, I'm there—costume or no costume. I'm all yours to do with as you wish."

This time, they sealed the deal with a kiss.

Coming next in the EagerBoyz series

<u>Eager For Three</u>

One boyfriend's too many, so there's no way he's going to end up with two.

Bailey Forsythe is a socialite. Photographed at all the best parties, he's only interested in one thing—fun. A relationship? Not a chance. There's no way he's ever going to succumb to a bout of feelings. Not now. Not ever.

EagerBoyz models Drake and Jackson are renowned for their competitive nature. They've never filmed together because even being in the same room is a challenge. When both men set their sights on Bailey, competition gets even fiercer. He might be happy to share, but they're not so sure.

After an explosive night where barriers come down, Bailey's convinced Drake and Jackson could be perfect together. He might not be interested in a relationship, but he's not averse to playing matchmaker with himself as bait. Only what happens when it's time to take himself out of the picture? Is he really as immune to emotional attachments as he makes out?

Maybe three into two really does go. But Bailey's going to take a hell of a lot of convincing. It's going to be the toughest competition Drake and Jackson have ever faced.

This time, though, they're in it together. Two against one. In the hope of making it three.

Thanks

Thanks for reading this book. If you can take the time to leave a review, I would really appreciate it.

H.L Day Special Access

WANT TO BE ABLE TO get your hands on stories that aren't available anywhere else?

Subscribe to the H.L Day newsletter. You can sign up here https://landing.mailerlite.com/webforms/landing/j7q6r7

or through my website https://hldayauthor.co.uk

Here you can find a link to bonus chapters from existing books as well as short stories that haven't been released anywhere else.

Get a 15k standalone fake relationship story **The Second Act**, the EagerBoyz prequel **Eager To Try**, and bonus material from both **Edge of Living** and **A Dance too Far** and **A Step too Far**.

Subscribing means you will be first in line for any new bonus material as well as receiving new release alerts, being eli-

EAGER FOR MORE

gible for newsletter-only giveaways and getting the most up-to-date information.

[Sign me up.][1]

Want even more up-to-date information? Then there's only one place for it, my FB group Day's Den where I post weekly teasers and excerpts of what I'm currently working on.

[Join the group.][2]

---

1. https://landing.mailerlite.com/webforms/landing/j7q6r7
2. https://www.facebook.com/groups/2214565008830022/?ref=bookmarks

About the Author

H.L DAY GREW UP IN the North of England. As a child she was an avid reader, spending lots of time at the local library or escaping into the imaginary worlds created by the books she read. Her grandmother first introduced her to the genre of romance novels, as a teenager, and all the steamy sex they entailed. Naughty Grandma!

One day, H.L Day stumbled upon the world of m/m romance. She remained content to read other people's books for a while, before deciding to give it a go herself.

Now, she's a teacher by day and a writer by night. Actually, that's not quite true—she's a teacher by day, procrastinates about writing at night and writes in the school holidays, when she's not continuing to procrastinate. After all, there's books to read, places to go, people to see, exercise at the gym to do, films to watch. So many things to do—so few hours to do it in. Every now and again, she musters enough self-discipline to actually get some words onto paper—sometimes they even make sense and are in the right order.

You can find H.L Day at the following places

Twitter[1].
Instagram[2]
Facebook.[3]

---

1. https://twitter.com/HLDAY100
2. https://www.instagram.com/h.l.day101/?hl=en

Send me a friend request or come and join my group -Day's Den[4] for the most up-to-date information and for the chance at receiving ARCs

[Website][5]

[Newsletter][6]

---

3. https://www.facebook.com/profile.php?id=100010513175490
4. https://www.facebook.com/groups/2214565008830022/?ref=bookmarks
5. https://hldayauthor.co.uk/
6. https://landing.mailerlite.com/webforms/landing/j7q6r7

More MM romance books by H.L Day

Romantic comedies

A Temporary Situation
A Christmas Situation
Temporary Insanity
Taking Love's Lead

Suspense

A Dance too Far
A Step too Far

Contemporary

Eager For More
Edge of Living
Kept in the Dark
Time for a Change
Christmas Riches

Postapocalyptic Sci-fi

Refuge

Read the blurb for these books through H.L Day's website[7] or on H.L Day's Amazon page[8].

---

7. https://hldayauthor.co.uk/
8. https://www.amazon.com/H-L-Day/e/B0768KF4K2?ref=sr_ntt_srch_lnk_2&qid=1580204625&sr=8-2

Available In audio

Kept in the Dark
Edge of Living
A Dance too Far
A Step too Far

If you like this book, you may also like

<u>Eager For You: A fake relationship gay romance. (EagerBoyz 1)</u>

Who better to fake it than two people who do it for a living?

Student Josh Keating, better known in the adult film world as Angel, has a problem. His family expects to meet his boyfriend that weekend. Except he doesn't have one. When fresh-faced newbie Leo Stone offers himself up to play the part, Josh finds it impossible to turn him down.

Damian Price has only masqueraded as Leo Stone for a couple of months so far, his decision to join the studio heavily influenced by the huge torch he carries for Angel. He might just be his biggest fan. So, of course he's going to jump at the chance to play his boyfriend for the weekend. As long as Josh doesn't get wind of Damian's true feelings or see through the little white lies he's been telling, everything will be fine.

One weekend.

One bed.

A growing mutual attraction.

An adult film star who's not above using his own performances for the purposes of seduction.

<u>Buy from Amazon</u>

Time for a Change: A Grumpy vs Sunshine gay romance

WHAT IF THE LAST THING you want, might be the very thing you need?

Stuffy and uptight accountant Michael's life is exactly the way he likes it: ordered, routine and risk-free. He doesn't need chaos and he doesn't need anything shaking it up and causing him anxiety. The only blot on the horizon is the small matter of getting his ex-boyfriend Christian back. That's exactly the type of man Michael goes for: cultured, suave and sophisticated.

Coffee shop employee Sam is none of those things. He's a ball of energy and happiness who thinks nothing of flaunting his half-naked muscular body and devastating smile in front of Michael when he's trying to work. He knows what he wants—and that's Michael. And no matter how much Michael tries to resist him, he's not going to take no for an answer.

Sam eventually chips through Michael's barriers and straight into his bed. But Michael's already made some questionable decisions that might just come back to haunt him. He's got some difficult choices to make if he's ever going to find love. And he might just find that he's too set in his ways to make the right ones quickly enough. If Michael's not careful, the best thing that's ever happened to him might just slip right through his fingers. Because even a patient man like Sam has his limits.

[Buy from Amazon](http://getbook.at/TimeforaChange)

Kept in the Dark: An escort gay romance

STRUGGLING ACTOR DEAN only escorts occasionally to pay the bills. So, his first instinct on being offered a job with a strange set of conditions is to turn it down. No date. Don't switch the lights on. Don't touch him. I mean, what's that all about? What's the man trying to hide? Dean certainly doesn't expect sex with a faceless stranger to spark so much passion inside him. It's just business though, right? He can put a stop to it whenever he wants.

When Dean meets Justin—a scarred, ex-army soldier unlucky in love. Dean's given a chance at a proper relationship. He can see past the scars to the man underneath. He's everything Dean could possibly wish for in a boyfriend: kind, caring and sweet. All Dean needs to do is be honest. Easy, right? But, Justin's holding back and Dean can't work out why. But whatever it is, it's enough to give him second thoughts.

They both have secrets which could shatter their fledgling relationship. After all, secrets have a nasty habit of coming out eventually. The question is when they do, will they be able to piece their relationship back together? Or will they be left with nothing but memories of bad decisions and the promise of the love they could have had, if only they'd both been honest and fought harder.

[Buy from Amazon][10]

[Also available in audio]

---

[10] http://getbook.at/KITD